PROTOTYPE

ALPHA-3

PROTOTYPE ALPHA-3

PROTOTYPE SERIES BOOK 1

ALANAH ANDREWS

First published by Deadset Press in 2019
www.alanahandrews.com

ISBN: 978-0-6484211-5-3

For my youngest son, Blake, who loves to read. May you always find magic within the pages of a book.

“I hope, or I could not live.”

— H.G. Wells, The Island of Doctor Moreau

CHAPTER 1

They came in the night.

At least, Alpha-3 was fairly certain that it was night-time. There were no windows in Zone One, but the lights along the corridor had been dimmed enough to cast long, murky shadows across the wall. It was possible, of course, that it wasn't night-time at all—perhaps the guards had turned the lights down simply because they felt like it. With no watch or clock in her cell, Alphie couldn't tell either way.

She lay on the thin mattress, staring up at the dark ceiling of her cell, when Zeta-7 called out from the far end of the corridor, "Quiet, someone's coming,"

Alphie didn't hear anything different at first. She held her breath, listening intently, thinking it was probably just one of the guards checking on the Zone One prototypes. There was a click as the door at the end of the corridor opened, and Alphie squeezed her eyes shut, pretending to be asleep. She didn't want to do anything to provoke the wrath of the guards.

"Which one is it?" asked a rough voice, as heavy footsteps clonked along the corridor.

"Cell Four," came the reply. Alphie recognised this voice—it was Michael, her least-favourite guard.

Cell Four. They had come for Delta-20. Of course they had. Alphie opened her eyes and rolled over, peering through the bars. A flash of light from a torch illuminated the corridor outside the cells.

"Delta-20. Hands."

Alphie crept slowly out of her bed, careful not to attract any unwanted attention. Shuffling closer to the bars, she could just make out two figures in the darkness outside Cell Four. A rattle of chains echoed around Zone One as the men worked to restrain Delta-20.

Not that they needed to bother. Delta-20 wasn't going to struggle. She was giggling, calling out to the other prototypes in a sing-song voice. "Goodbye, everyone. I bet you didn't think that I'd be next."

But Alphie *had* guessed that Delta would be next to leave Zone One. It was always the Deltas who got to leave. Sure, every now and then an Epsilon or a Gamma would go, but more often than not, it was a Delta. *And,* thought Alphie, bitterly, *it was never, ever an Alpha.*

"Shut it," said Michael, "unless you'd like a final sting from the stun-band."

Delta was quiet then, as the guard unlocked Cell Four and led Delta-20 out into the corridor. Alphie gazed at Delta-20's retreating back with jealousy. She wasn't surprised that another Delta was getting out of here, but that didn't make it any easier to accept. Meanwhile, Alpha-3 was stuck at AWPA for another day, week, month, or year, praying that she could do enough for Genocorp to finally notice her.

CHAPTER 2

The helicopter nosedived towards the landing pad, and Carmen gripped the sides of her seat hard enough to make her knuckles ache. From the air, the island looked deceptively small, dominated by the grey-and-brown buildings of AWPA's offshore testing facility.

Of course, the lab itself was like an iceberg—only the tip was visible to the eye, and the rest was tucked out of sight, underground. The helicopter landed with a small bump, and Carmen scurried out the door, dragging her suitcase with her. The pilot gave her a small salute and—barely waiting for her to clear the landing zone—took off back to the mainland. Carmen held her coat close to her body as the rotor blades churned the air like a mini-tornado.

Her phone beeped, and she pulled it out of her pocket, checking her emails as she dragged her bag along the path to the front reception.

From: <Greenwood.Lucinda@awpa.mil >
To: <Rhodes.Carmen@awpa.mil>
Attachments: 1

Subject: Testing schedule 4 June – 8 June

Testing schedule attached.

Lucinda

Carmen rolled her eyes. No 'Hi Carmen,' or 'Good morning,' or 'How was your weekend?' That wasn't Lucinda's way. 'Testing schedule attached' contained more words than some of the emails the lead scientist on Project Chrysalis had sent to Carmen.

Reaching the main reception, Carmen passed her suitcase over to the man behind the desk. He smiled at her, promising to have the luggage taken up to her room straight away. Carmen gave him a nod, downloading the testing schedule and checking the list for Monday. First up, she would be working with Alpha-3, then onto Gamma-11 and Zeta-7. Carmen felt herself relax— a day without assessing Delta-20 was a good day indeed.

Swiping her finger across her screen, Carmen looked at the schedule for Tuesday and frowned. Then she moved across to Wednesday and Thursday, before putting her phone in her pocket. Perhaps Lucinda had decided that she wanted to work with the difficult prototype herself, which was fine with Carmen. If Lucinda felt that she could do any better with Delta-20, she was welcome to try.

Gripping her laptop case, Carmen took the elevator down two levels. "Goodbye, sun," she muttered to no-one, as the doors closed behind her.

She wasn't sure if spending the weekend at home on the mainland had improved her mood about being at work, or just made it worse.

The elevator deposited her near the main dining room, and as Carmen walked across to the Secure Area, she waved at the cooks in the kitchen. "Morning," she called out in greeting, and a couple waved back. A delicious smell made Carmen's stomach rumble, and she realised that the only thing she'd had for breakfast was a cup of coffee.

There was no time to stop now, though, so she told her stomach to have some patience as she swiped her ID beneath the scanner on the eastern wall. The door opened with a high-pitched beep. On the other side of the door, a long corridor stretched out before her.

Stepping inside the Secure Area, she took a small, black remote from its holster on the wall and attached the retractable cord to her belt. Then she unlocked the first door to her left, marked with a large white number one.

When she entered Zone One, the first thing Carmen noticed was that Cell Four appeared to be empty. Making sure that she was staying on the far side of the yellow line painted on the floor, Carmen peered into the cell, checking to see whether the prototype was in its bed, or perhaps hiding in a corner. Looks could be deceiving when it came to the Alpha models, so she reached for the clipboard hanging on the wall opposite the cell to see if anybody had taken the prototype out of the area. The clipboard wasn't there.

"She's gone," said a small voice from further along the corridor. Carmen rested her hand lightly on the stun-band regulator attached to her belt and walked along to Cell One. A small prototype with dark eyes looked up at her from its bed. "They took her last night."

"Who took the prototype?" asked Carmen. "Was it a woman with grey hair?"

Alpha-3 shook her head. "No. It was a guy in black. Looked like the same one who took Delta-19."

Carmen nodded, slowly. In some universe, she supposed that it must make sense that the Delta models were so quickly selected to leave, when she herself thought they were fairly average.

"When will Delta-21 arrive?" asked Alpha-3, sliding off its bed and standing up.

Carmen checked that the yellow line was still in front of her toes. "I'm not sure," she replied.

"Are you here to assess me?" asked Alpha-3.

"Yes."

The prototype nodded, its face thoughtful. "I'm going to do well today, Miss. No stopping until I've reached my full potential."

"That's the spirit," said Carmen, reaching for her radio.

"You don't need to call a guard," said Alpha-3. "I won't do anything wrong. You know that I wouldn't hurt you." Its brown eyes looked up at her, and Carmen could almost—almost—fool herself that it was human.

"It's protocol," replied Carmen, holding down the button on side of the transceiver and lifting it to her lips. "Assistance to Zone One."

There was a crackle of static. "Yes, Carmen?"

"Hey, Scott, you wanna help me transport a prototype to the Examination Room?"

"No problem, I'll be right there." The static grew louder, then the line went silent.

"I did good last week, didn't I, Miss Carmen?" asked Alpha-3, staring through the bars.

"Oh yes," said Carmen, "very good. You progressed more last week than you have in months."

The prototype beamed up at her. "Do you think I'll be getting out of here soon, then?"

Carmen thought about it for a moment. It was hard to predict when GenoCorp would decide that they wanted one of the prototypes. Some, like Zeta-7, she thought they would have taken months ago. The prototype's hearing range was incredible, really, and every time Carmen worked with it, the prototype would be able to hear another frequency beyond normal human range.

And yet, after all this time, Zeta-7 was still there in Cell Six.

"I'm sure you will," said Carmen, "if you keep improving the way you did last week."

"And what about Beta-6?"

"What about Beta-6?" asked Carmen, raising an eyebrow.

"The thing is, if I'm getting out soon . . . well, I'd like to know that Beta-6 was getting out around the same time. You know, so we could go to GenoCorp together."

"Oh," said Carmen, realisation dawning on her. It seemed that the prototypes had enough humanity to form attachments, at least. Then again, animals sought companionship in the same way. "Well, yes," she said, carefully, "I think Beta-6 is getting close to release as well. It'll probably only be a few weeks after you, if it keeps working hard."

"He, not it," said Alpha-3, smiling. "Thank you, Miss Carmen. I'll try harder. Today, and tomorrow, and the day after. I will prove myself. And then—"

"Shhh Alpha-3," said Carmen, raising a finger to her lips. "Let's focus on today for a start."

***

Carmen gazed down at the data she had recorded over the past two hours and gave a low whistle. She'd been working with Alpha-3 for a long time, and yet, in the past, its decoding abilities had progressed at a negligible level. All until the final session last week.

Today, the prototype had done even better than on Friday, successfully identifying patterns and solving code in not one, but three data sets.

Opposite her, the prototype sat silently in its wheelchair, eyes closed. "Did I do okay, Miss?" It gave a large yawn.

"You did fine, Alpha-3."

The prototype opened its eyes, shifting as much as it could beneath the bonds adhering it to the wheelchair. It flexed its hands against the straps restraining its wrists. "Just fine?"

Carmen couldn't help smiling. Pushing the documents they had used throughout the session across the table, she tapped a finger in the centre of the top one. "This one took you forty-five minutes to solve. A month ago—hell, even a week ago—you would have spent the entire two hours on it and maybe, maybe worked it out." She spread the pages apart, fanning them out on the desk. "This one, half an hour. And this one,"—she pointed at the most recent data set—"only took you twenty minutes. Twenty. And you got them all right."

Alpha-3 yawned again, and Carmen realised just how much of a toll it had taken on the prototype. It might be showing progress, but she needed to be mindful of its mental wellbeing. Push it too far, or too fast, and it could all go backwards in no time—she'd seen it happen before.

"Anyway," said Carmen, collecting the sheets and placing them in a brown file, "we'd better get you back to your cell."

"Miss Carmen?"

"Yes, Alpha-3?"

"Have you stopped recording now?"

Carmen raised an eyebrow. "Yes, the cameras are off."

"Oh, good. Can you tell me a story?"

Carmen smiled, closing down her laptop and placing it into her bag, along with the file on Alpha-3. "I suppose," she said. "One I've told you before, or a new one?"

The prototype thought for a moment, wriggling in its wheelchair. It must be uncomfortable, thought Carmen, being stuck sitting down for so long like that. And then she checked her thoughts. It was too easy to view the prototypes as human, too easy to forget their true potential. In the training videos, she'd seen exactly what a prototype could do to a quality assurance assessor.

"I liked Pinocchio. And Cinderella. You could tell me one of those again. Just not Hansel and Gretel. I didn't like that one."

"And why's that?" asked Carmen.

The prototype shrugged. "The parents kicked the kids out. That was pretty awful. And then the witch locked them up . . ."

Carmen almost laughed. Perhaps that particular fairy tale hit a little close to home. Maybe Miss Carmen was the witch.

"Actually, maybe I'd like a new one," said Alpha-3.

Carmen thought about the stories that she'd already told the prototype. All of Danielle's favourite ones—*Cinderella, Sleeping Beauty, Snow White*—had been shared a long time ago. On a whim, she'd put one of her daughter's old books in her luggage before returning to AWPA, but it would be securely stowed in her room by now.

Carmen tapped her finger on her arm, thinking. Next time, she would have to make sure she brought the book down to the testing rooms to jog her memory.

"Oh," she said at last, "would you like to hear about a king who wishes to turn everything into gold?"

"Sure," said Alpha-3.

Lucinda would probably frown upon Carmen telling the prototype fairy stories—any interaction that wasn't directly related to its assessment was to be discouraged, in Lucinda's eyes. And yet, it was Carmen's job to get results. Her methods might involve less pain—and more fairy tales—than the other assessors, but that didn't mean that she wasn't doing a good job.

Alpha-3 closed its eyes and Carmen sat back in her chair, recalling the story. It was nice, in a way, to be able to tell these tales again—her own children were far too old to want to hear about *King Midas*.

"Once upon a time," prompted Alpha-3.

"Once upon a time," repeated Carmen, "there was a greedy king called Midas, and everything he touched turned to gold."

CHAPTER 3

"Alphie?"

There was a sharp tapping sound on the metal grate beside Alpha-3's bed and she rolled over, yawning.

"Are you awake?"

"Mmm," replied Alphie, raising herself onto her knees and peering through the small holes in the metal. "Just."

"You slept through dinner."

Alphie looked down at the floor, where a plastic tray of cold food sat waiting for her.

"How did you go?"

Alphie stretched, feeling the stiffness in her limbs gradually dissipate. "Fine. Great, actually. Miss Carmen says I'm improving."

There was a small shuffling sound on the other side of the wall as Beta-6 put his mouth up to the grate. "That's fantastic, Alphie, well done."

Alphie could feel the warmth of Beta's breath on her cheek as he spoke through the cool metal. The heat seemed to travel from her cheek and spread through her chest as she imagined herself and Beta-6 on the outside. Beta's reddish-blonde hair—long, of course, because there were no mandatory haircuts on the outside—rippled on an imaginary sea breeze as she clasped his hand in her own. "When's your next assessment?" she asked.

"Not until tomorrow."

"Did you hear what Miss Carmen said earlier? About you and me and GenoCorp?"

"Yeah, I heard."

Alphie sat with her back against the wall, looking around her small cell. She knew every inch of it, every mark in the concrete, every tiny camera hidden in the walls. "Can you imagine what it's like outside AWPA?"

Beta was silent, and Alpha-3 wondered if she appeared in his dreams of the outside, just as he did in hers.

"When I get out," said a deep voice from further along the corridor, "I hope I get to be in a nice big house. Nothing small like this cell."

"I don't think it needs to be big," Alphie replied to Epsilon, "but I do want it to be really bright. And it's not going to have any locks. Actually, maybe it won't even have doors."

"I'd like doors," said Epsilon, "so that I could take a dump without anyone watching me."

Alphie laughed and glanced up at the camera on the wall, a red light on the front like an all-seeing eye.

"I think I'd like a garden," said Beta, slowly. "When I've done assessments outside, I've smelt the sea breeze and seen trees and plants and grass. I want something like that."

The other prototypes murmured in agreement. Trees, gardens, flowers—it sounded nice. Normal.

Human.

"I think I'd like us to be together," said Zeta-7, from the cell at the far end of the corridor. "All of us in a big house where we could see each other whenever we wanted."

"I'm not sure that's how it works," said Alphie, practically.

"I don't care," said Zeta, her voice more heated than usual. "It's what I want."

"We could have mirrors," said Gamma, excitedly.

"And parents."

"I don't want parents," said Epsilon. "I don't want anyone telling me what to do any more."

Alphie didn't agree with him. She wanted parents, and every time she closed her eyes and imagined them, they looked a lot like Miss Carmen. "You don't think GenoCorp is going to tell us what to do?"

"I suppose they will," said Beta, "but it'll be different from here. We'll have missions and stuff. We won't have to constantly try to prove ourselves."

The Zone One prototypes fell silent, lost in their dreams of the future, and Alphie retrieved her tray of food from the floor. It might be cold, but she was suddenly starving. "When do you think the new Delta will arrive?" she asked between bites of cold mashed potato.

"I dunno," said Beta. "No-one was probably expecting GenoCorp to take Delta-20 so quickly. Might be a while."

"Maybe," said Alphie, "I mean, if they only create one prototype at a time, on an as-needed basis."

"Isn't that how you said it works?" asked Beta.

Alphie shrugged, and then remembered that as good as Beta's eyesight was, he still couldn't see through walls. "I said it's how I think it *might* work," said Alphie. Information about where the prototypes came from was scarce, patched together from small snippets gained from conversations with Miss Carmen, or overheard between the guards. They were always tight-lipped when it came to any questions asked by the prototypes. Sit down. Shut up. Excel at the tests. That was the general mantra. "Or maybe," said Alphie, thinking aloud, "they just have all the prototypes in reserve, already grown and modified and ready to be tested. Then they just have to wake them up."

The thought seemed to intrigue Beta-6. "What, like sitting on ice or something?"

"Maybe," said Alphie again. "I mean, it's not like we remember anything before being here, so we could have been on ice, or in suspended animation or something."

"Suspended what?"

"Suspended animation. I read about it in one of the data sets that Miss Carmen had me decode. You like, don't breathe but you're still—"

A piercing pain rocketed through Alphie's neck and she cried out, falling back on the bed, food crashing to the ground.

Similar grunts and moans of pain echoed around Zone One as Alphie writhed on the bed, willing the stream of hurt flowing into her neck to stop. She held her hands up to the cool band around her throat. Stupid, so stupid—she had been so caught up in their conversation, that she hadn't even considered that one of the guards might be listening in, or watching them on the cameras.

The door at the end of the corridor clicked open, and there was a clop of shoes on concrete as the guard approached. Alphie's entire being was so focused on the pain that she hardly even noticed Michael until he was right outside her cell, staring in. His eyes were black holes, boring into her.

Pressing a button on the regulator hanging at his hip, the pain stopped as abruptly as it had begun, and Alphie lay panting on the bed, covered in sweat. The guard watched her without any emotion on his face.

"Pleased with yourself, are you?" he asked in a low voice, full of menace. "Keep up the chat and I'll activate all the stun-bands again, and then I might just go and make myself a cup of coffee. Got it?"

Alphie nodded, not daring to speak. As the click of the guard's feet moved back down the hallway, Alphie wiped a single tear from her face that must have escaped during the episode. Sniffing, she got up and tried to sweep the food off the floor and back onto the tray.

CHAPTER 4

"Again."

Carmen stifled a yawn as Zeta-7 closed its eyes, concentrating on the sounds flowing through the headphones. The week hadn't been too bad, all things considered. Alpha-3 was definitely the standout—making advances in leaps and bounds—but most of the other prototypes in Zone One had been able to make some sort of progress. Not having to work with a Delta all week had definitely raised Carmen's spirits.

She watched Zeta-7 closely as the prototype sat still, listening intently to the recording. There was no reaction on the prototype's pale face, no twitch or hint that the prototype could hear anything. Carmen noted this down on the document in front of her.

The door to the Examination Room swung silently open and Scott appeared, framed in the doorway. Carmen gave him a little wave and raised a finger to her lips. He nodded, waiting for the test to be over.

"I know you're there," said Zeta-7, without opening its eyes. "Scott. I can hear your heartbeat."

Carmen cleared her throat. "How do you know it's Scott's heartbeat?"

The prototype winced and Carmen leant forward, adjusting the knob on the side of the headset to increase the soundproofing.

"Scott's average heart rate is slower than the other guards," explained Zeta, "and then every third or fourth beat, there's a little *whoosh* that nobody else has."

The guard laughed and took a couple of steps into the room. "Who needs a doctor when I've got Zeta-7?" he said, smiling. "Guess I'd better get that looked at."

"Never mind that," said Carmen. "Could you hear anything in the last test?"

The prototype shook its head.

"Okay, Zeta-7, that's it for today. You're rostered on for one more assessment tomorrow afternoon, and then you're done for the week." *And then I get to go home.*

"Could you please turn the soundproofing up?" asked Zeta-7.

"More?"

Zeta-7 nodded. "All the way, if possible. I'd love some silence."

Carmen adjusted the knob on the side of the headset and the prototype visibly relaxed, closing its eyes.

"Is it doing well, then?" asked Scott, as Carmen put her laptop in her bag. "Making good progress?"

"Slow and steady," replied Carmen.

"You think GenoCorp will take it soon?"

Carmen shrugged, standing up. "Who knows with GenoCorp. I would never have guessed that Delta-20 would be gone so soon."

Scott looked at her with a strange expression.

"What?"

He shrugged, clasping the handles of the wheelchair and pushing it towards the door.

"Scott," said Carmen, "we've known each other for years. Are you telling me Delta-20 didn't go to GenoCorp after all?"

Silence. He glanced at the prototype sitting in the wheelchair.

"The soundproofing on its headphones is turned right up," said Carmen. "It can't hear you."

"Delta-20 was too unpredictable," he said at last, turning back towards her. "Lucinda ordered its retirement."

"Are you serious?" said Carmen. "That was *my* prototype, and she just . . ." Carmen took a few deep breaths.

"I'm surprised she didn't tell you," said Scott, and the expression on his face did truly seem apologetic. "I thought you knew."

Carmen ran a hand across her face, shaking her head.

"Never mind," said Scott, "the new Delta will be here soon enough."

"Mmhmm," said Carmen.

Scott looked like he wanted to say something else, then changed his mind, pushing the wheelchair out into the corridor.

Sitting back down at the table in the centre of the room, Carmen retrieved her phone from her bag and dialled Lucinda.

"This is Lucinda, leave a mess—"

Carmen hung up. She was certainly *not* going to leave a message about something as important as this. Instead, she scrolled through her contacts and called the head of Project Chrysalis, John Haven—Lucinda's superior, even if he didn't seem to know it.

"Carmen, how are you?"

"Are you on site, John?"

"Yes, I—"

"I'd like to speak to you. In person."

There was a brief silence as though he was considering her request. "I wanted to see you about something anyway," he said at last. "I'll be in my office in ten minutes."

***

John wasn't alone when Carmen arrived at his office. A woman with grey flecks in her tight bun was sitting opposite him at the desk.

John stood up, gesturing for Carmen to take a seat. "Lucinda noticed that she had a missed call from you, so I suggested that she join us," said John, "if that's okay?"

Carmen shut the door behind her. "It's fine." She slipped into the proffered seat, moving it a few inches away from the stern woman.

"So," said John, "what did you want to speak to us about?"

Carmen took a deep breath. "What happened to Delta-20?"

John raised an eyebrow, then nodded towards Lucinda to answer.

"Delta-20 was retired," said Lucinda. "Is that all?"

Carmen bristled. "I thought it was taken by GenoCorp."

"Well, you jumped to that conclusion all by yourself."

"You didn't correct me."

The head scientist turned in her seat so that she could look Carmen directly in the eye. "You are a quality assurance assessor, Professor Rhodes. You test the prototypes. That is all. You don't need to know more than that."

"You killed my prototype!"

Lucinda raised an eyebrow. "*Your* prototype? They belong to AWPA. Not to mention that they are *prototypes*, Carmen. Samples. Models. And if they aren't up to scratch they are retired—"

"Killed."

"No, retired. You can kill a human. You can kill an animal. These prototypes are neither, and we have the complete right to do whatever we want to with them." Lucinda turned towards John. "Professor Haven, I don't have time for this."

John waved his hand in the air. "Go, go. I'm sure you have plenty of work to do."

"No," said Carmen, standing up. "Lucinda, you can't just retire my prototypes without consulting me. I work with them every day—I know the Zone One prototypes better than anyone here. I might be able to see potential that isn't clear simply from the results."

Lucinda and John were both quiet. "Very well," said Lucinda, "so, in your *expertise*, which prototype is demonstrating the most progress right now?"

Carmen thought for a moment, ignoring the sneer in Lucinda's voice. "Alpha-3," she said at last. "Over the past week, it has demonstrated enhanced decoding abilities, far outstripping its results thus far."

"Very well," said Lucinda, rising from her seat. "John, I'll send you a new testing schedule for Carmen in a few minutes."

"A new testing schedule? What—?" Carmen seethed as Lucinda left the office.

"Sit down, Carmen," said John, "there's a few things that I wanted to talk to you about."

"What sort of things? John, maybe we could have got somewhere with Delta-20, if you'd given me the chance."

"Delta-20 was retired due to not meeting our benchmarks. I think you will find that Delta-21 will be much more promising. Which is exactly what I wanted to talk to you about."

***

Carmen pushed the door harder than she needed to as she entered her bedroom, and it made a loud bang as it collided with the wall. She imagined that it was John's head instead of a wall. Or Lucinda's head. That made her feel slightly better.

Throwing her new assessment schedule onto the bed, she reached for the bottle of wine sitting on her dresser.

"Frickin' John," she muttered under her breath, steeling herself for the awkward phone-call she was about to make. She poured herself a drink, downed it in two large gulps, then poured herself another one before dialling her ex-husband's number.

"You've reached Patrick, Danielle and Marcus. We can't come to the phone right now. Please leave a message after the beep."

Carmen waited.

"Haha, fooled you. Leave a message after this beep."

Such a professional answerphone. "Hey, Patrick. It's Carmen. Unfortunately, something's come up at work and I won't be able to have the kids this weekend. I hope you understand . . . please apologise to them for me, and I'll see them next weekend. Bye."

She hung up the phone, feeling guilty, but leaving a message was definitely a lot better than having to speak to her ex-husband.

She smoothed out the wrinkles in the assessment schedule that John had given her, noting the increased frequency of assessments for the Alpha-model. Of course, Alpha-3's improvements weren't the main reason that she had been directed to remain at AWPA over the weekend.

"Here's to the new Delta," Carmen murmured, draining her wine glass.

It was going to be a long week.

CHAPTER 5

"The new Delta is here."

When Zeta-7 whispered the news, Alphie pressed against the bars of her cell, peering out into the corridor. Lamenting the fact that her cell was the furthest from the main entrance to Zone One, Alphie squeezed herself into the corner as far as she could, looking across towards the door.

The whole zone held its breath, as though even the concrete walls were waiting, trembling with anticipation. Just as Alphie thought that perhaps Zeta had been mistaken, the door clicked open.

The new prototype was wheeled into Zone One, but all Alphie could see was the side of its wheelchair and a leg covered in loose orange pants. Female or male? Alphie couldn't tell, but then again, what did that matter?

"Mornin'," said a man with a coarse voice, "where do you want it?"

"Cell Four," came Michael's reply. "Is it adequately sedated?"

There was a grunt from the other man. "It started waking as we got it out of the chopper, but it's in no condition to be doing much."

Michael's laughter echoed oddly around Zone One, bouncing off the walls and into Alphie's cell. She crossed her arms, leaning into the cold bars.

"I have experience with the Delta models—I'm not taking any chances." There was a clopping of feet on concrete, and then Michael's voice, low and mean. "You see this button, Prototype? If I press this, you'll get a shock so painful it'll make your eyes water. And then if I touch this dial, the pain will get even stronger until finally, your body won't be able to handle it. If you put so much as one finger out of line, I won't hesitate to use it. Got it?"

There was no response, but Michael must have been satisfied because a moment later there was the sound of a cell door opening, a click as the wheelchair released its captive, and then another clang as the cell was closed firmly behind the newly arrived prototype.

"I'll need you to sign some paperwork," came the rough voice again.

"No problem," said Michael. "Let's head out into the cafeteria—better light."

The door closed behind them, and the prototypes were left alone to meet the new arrival. There was no point in staying near the bars, so Alphie lay on her bed, running a finger along the pockmarked wall separating her from Beta.

"Hello," Gamma's wispy voice trickled through the cells. "Are you awake?"

There was a shuffle of movement and then silence.

"I know it's strange," continued Gamma, her voice light and airy, "but you'll get used to it. I'm Gamma. If you look through the grate on your wall you might be able to see me."

"Go away."

Alphie smiled, tracing the bumps on the wall in a figure-eight pattern. It seemed that Delta-21 was going to be just as feisty and rude as Delta-20.

"We understand," came Epsilon's deep voice. "We've all been where you are now. We all know how scary it is to arrive at Zone One and have no idea who you are or why you are here."

There was a creak of mattress springs. "I'm not scared." The new Delta's words slurred slightly, probably from the sedative. "I'm angry."

"And that's fine too," said Epsilon. "Just don't let the anger cloud your judgment."

Delta gave a short laugh, more like a bark. "And who are you?"

"I'm Epsilon-10, on the other side of you." There was the sound of tapping on metal. "Over here."

"Ten?" asked the new Delta. "That's a strange name."

A few wry chuckles punctured the air.

"Your name is Delta-21," explained Epsilon. "You are a prototype in AWPA, the Advanced Weaponised Projects Agency."

"No, I'm not." Her voice was getting stronger now. Perhaps the sedatives were starting to wear off. The shock of waking up in a small cell with no idea who you were was enough to sober anyone up pretty quickly.

"Sorry to break it to you, hun," said Zeta, from the furthest cell, "but you are. You're the twenty-first prototype in the Delta series."

"Don't call me *hun*," said Delta-21. "And I don't even know what that means. What do you mean twenty-first? Where are the other twenty?" Her voice was getting higher—she was starting to panic.

"Gone," said Alphie. She had never got along with Delta-20—or Delta-19, for that matter—but with an entire five possible friends in the world, not counting Miss Carmen, she was willing to do what she could to start their relationship off on the right foot.

"Lucky them. Where did they go?"

"GenoCorp. It's why they created you—created all of us— to *exceed the human potential*."

"You're talking bull," said Delta, and there was a clang as though she had hit the bars of her cell. "You're all talking bull."

"Sorry," said Gamma, "but it's the truth. This is Zone One. Your home."

Home. Alphie almost laughed. There were little things she did to try to make the empty cell a little more personal, like scratching tiny marks into the walls, but it would never really be a *home*. No, her first home would be when she finally joined GenoCorp. *If* she ever joined GenoCorp.

"Shut up," said Delta-21, her voice getting louder, "all of you, just shut up. This is *not* my home."

Alphie heard the new prototype flop down on her bed.

"Okay," said Gamma, "we'll stop talking about it. Alphie, maybe you should tell us one of your stories? They always make me feel better. What's the one with the prince?"

"Most of them have princes," said Alphie, smiling. "And princesses. And happy endings." That was the best part of the fairy tale stories that Miss Carmen told her. The endings.

"Okay, the one with the glass shoe."

"Cinderella? Sure." Alphie lay back and gazed up at the roof, seeing instead a young girl covered in ashes, cleaning out a fireplace. As she began the story, Zone One fell into silence, punctuated every now and then by quiet sobs from Cell Four.

CHAPTER 6

Carmen entered Zone One with her laptop bag in one hand and the other clasped around a half-empty coffee cup. After a few too many wines last night, her stomach had protested against eating breakfast this morning. Coffee, however, seemed to be doing the trick.

Scott met her at the door. Whereas Michael was all lines and sharp edges—in personality, as well as physique—Scott was the opposite. Shorter, rounder, and with a soft voice, Scott always reminded her of a grandfather she had never met.

"How's the new prototype?" Carmen asked, taking a sip of her coffee.

"I just got here, Professor," said Scott, "and so far Delta-21 has been sleeping. You want to test it now?"

"No," said Carmen, "I'm working with Alpha-3 first."

Scott reached for the regulator tethered to his belt. Holding it in front of him, he fiddled with the dials and then strode past the prototypes to the far end of the corridor.

Carmen followed along behind. As she passed Cell Four, she glanced in curiously to see the new Delta, but it was still in bed, the grey blanket covering its body. No matter, she would become acquainted with the newest prototype soon enough.

The jingle of keys from Scott's belt drew Alpha-3 forward in the last cell, and it looked at Carmen curiously. "Good morning, Scott. Good morning, Miss Carmen," said the prototype, stifling a yawn. "Did I sleep through the weekend?"

"No, Alpha-3, it's still Friday."

"Wrists," said the guard, and Alpha-3 poked both hands through the gaps in the bars. Scott scanned the tattoo on its left wrist—not unlike scanning groceries at the supermarket on the mainland—and then ordered the prototype to turn around. "Everything seems in order, Ms Rhodes," he said, inspecting the stun-band around the prototype's neck. "Ready?"

Carmen awkwardly dragged the wheelchair with one hand towards the cell. With a curt nod, Scott unlocked the door and then stepped back, holding the small regulator in clear view.

Carmen had another sip of coffee and stepped behind the older man, watching carefully as Alpha-3 moved out of its cell and into the hallway, taking a seat in the wheelchair. Scott's finger hovered over the button in the centre of the regulator as Alpha-3 leaned into the armrests of the wheelchair, causing the clamps to lock tightly around its arms and legs.

The process was probably a little over-the-top for Alpha-3. After all, the prototype had never shown any sort of violent tendencies. However, protocol was protocol. Carmen flushed slightly, well aware that obeying the rules wasn't always her greatest strength.

With the prototype firmly locked into the chair, Scott released the regulator and it zipped backwards, dangling from his belt. "You want backup?"

She shook her head, checking that her radio and regulator were safely attached to her belt. "This one'll be fine. I might need assistance with the new Delta, though." Carmen hung her laptop bag over the handles and pushed the wheelchair towards the open door, propping her coffee cup against the back of the chair.

"Uhh, Miss?"

Carmen stopped as the red light on Alpha-3's stun-band began to flash and emit a high-pitched beep. "Oh, damn." Retrieving the regulator, Carmen flicked the switch that removed the locater restriction on the stun-band and the flashing light disappeared. She gave an apologetic grin towards Scott. "Whoops, I'm really not with it this morning. See you in a couple of hours." She pushed the prototype along the corridor towards Examination Room Two.

"Miss, I thought you said I was done with testing for this week."

"You were," said Carmen, positioning the wheelchair beside the table in the centre of the room. Reaching into her bag, she retrieved the transparent screen that had appeared in her pigeon-hole this morning. "But things change."

The prototype frowned, looking upset.

"This is a good thing, Alpha-3," said Carmen, as she attached the screen to the side of the wheelchair, adjusting it so that it was at eye-level with the prototype.

"What's that?" asked Alpha-3, its dark eyes wide as it stared at the screen.

"A new way of testing you."

"Okay . . . and why's it a good thing?"

Carmen's finger's twitched. The prototypes knew that they weren't supposed to ask questions—would probably never try this with a guard. Maybe she was too soft on all of them. She was *definitely* too soft on Alpha-3.

Carmen pulled the laptop out of her bag and sat down at a seat on the other side of the table, draining her coffee cup with a satisfied sigh. "It means you're getting closer to GenoCorp. The frequency of testing will increase, as will the nature of the tests—as you'll see in a moment."

Carmen downloaded the latest test from the AWPA sharepoint and activated the program. A series of letters appeared simultaneously on her laptop and on the screen attached to the wheelchair.

"Woah," said Alpha-3, eyes wide as she stared at the screen.

"As you can see," explained Carmen, "this way, we can easily increase the quantity and speed of the data being shown to you."

"No more paper? Or books?"

"No more paper or books," confirmed Carmen. "The rate at which you can decode the data has surpassed books, I'm afraid."

"I like books," said Alpha-3, "but okay. Is this what happened with Alpha-2 as well? Before he got taken by GenoCorp?"

"You ask a lot of questions," said Carmen. "Shh, let's start."

A waterfall of text began to flow down the screen and Carmen walked across to the box on the wall, turning on the video cameras.

Over the next hour, the prototype unjumbled letters and numbers with ease. Carmen took copious notes, writing down everything the prototype said and did. It saw patterns where Carmen saw none, and she was sure that John—and GenoCorp—were going to be impressed. It was almost worth having to miss her weekend at home. Almost.

Near the end of the second hour, the prototype began to yawn. "Just one more," said Carmen, downloading and activating another test sequence. "I know you're tired, but you've been doing so well. Just one more."

The prototype nodded, flexing its hands and legs against the wheelchair restraints. "Okay, Miss."

A new data set appeared on the screen and Carmen sat back, watching with interest. The prototype yawned again, and then sat up straighter, peering into the screen. Its eyes flicked left and right, left and right, taking in the letters and symbols in front of it. After a moment, it began to speak.

"Negative thirty-eight point—ouch!"

It took a moment for Carmen to realise that the *ouch* wasn't part of the data the prototype was decoding.

"Are you okay?" asked Carmen, pausing the program.

The prototype screwed up its eyes, frowning. "I saw a flash of light and then . . . I've just got a bit of a headache, I'm okay."

Carmen noticed the sheen of sweat on the prototype's face and decided to call it. "We're done for the day, Alpha-3. Well done, you did a good job."

The prototype smiled, clearly relieved at not having to push through another test.

"Do you want me to tell you another story?" asked Carmen, as she finished her notes. "You did well today, you deserve it."

The prototype thought for a moment and then nodded, wincing slightly.

"Which one?" asked Carmen.

"Well, Miss, with the new Delta arriving I've just been thinking a bit about . . . Can you tell me the one about when I was born?"

Carmen raised an eyebrow, closing her laptop and stowing it in her bag. "You weren't born, Alpha-3. You know that."

"Okay," said the prototype, "the one about me being created."

Carmen shrugged, thinking back over the basic information she had been given about the origin of the prototypes. Genetic engineering definitely wasn't her area of expertise. "Once upon a time there was a very clever scientist," she said at last. "She mashed together some DNA and created prototypes with human characteristics, but inhuman abilities. The end."

Alpha-3 stared off into the distance. "Have you been there, Miss Carmen? Where they create us?"

Carmen shook her head, standing up. "No, it's not in my jurisdiction."

"Why don't we remember any of it, Miss?" asked the prototype. "I think back as far as I can, but the only memories I have are of Zone One."

"I don't know," said Carmen. "Maybe there's not a lot to remember. Or maybe it's better not to remember. It must be painful to be grown in a lab."

"I suppose," said Alpha-3. The prototype yawned again, and Carmen picked up the radio.

"Scott? Alpha-3 is ready for collection."

CHAPTER 7

For a long time, Alphie lay on her bed drifting in and out of sleep. One moment, she would be in a dream world where princes and princesses roamed the land, and the next moment the scene would be replaced by the cold greyness of her cell.

"Alphie?"

Alphie fought unsuccessfully against the lure of the castle perched high on top of the rocky cliff, overlooking the sea. Alphie was the princess in the tower with long golden hair—all princesses had long hair, not shaved heads—and the knight arriving to save her was Beta-6.

There was a sharp tap on the metal grate between her cell and the next. "Alphie, are you okay?"

She opened her eyes. Her body felt heavy and the headache was still there. "Yes," she said quietly. "I think so."

"What happened to you?" asked Beta. "Miss Carmen seemed worried, but I couldn't talk until the guards left."

The fact that Beta was concerned about her ignited a small fire in Alphie's stomach. She rolled onto her side, imagining Beta's body in the same position on the other side of the wall. They were so close, really—except for the concrete wall in between them. "I got a headache during the test. It was pretty bad. Still is."

"Maybe you should tell the guards. Get some painkillers or something."

"Yeah, right."

Alphie heard a shuffle on the other side of the wall, and she imagined Beta-6 sitting up in bed, leaning against the wall, his reddish-blonde stubble poking out of his skull. His hair was the colour that she imagined the sunset might look like if she ever got to leave.

She ran a hand through the stubble on her own head. Everyone in Zone One had a few centimetres of hair these days. They used to be shaved regularly on bathing day, but not anymore. Now they were lucky to be shaved once every few weeks. It was like the prototypes in Zone One had become an afterthought—only the guards and Miss Carmen were invested in their progress.

Alphie thought about Michael's emotionless face as he activated the stun-band. Not even the guards seemed to care about the wellbeing of the prototypes anymore. She needed to prove herself to GenoCorp and get out of here before one of them went too far.

"Beta," said Alphie slowly, aware that their time for open conversation might be mere seconds before the guard re-entered Zone One. "Do you ever see things?"

The other prototype laughed, and Alphie enjoyed listening to the sound. "You're kidding, right? I see everything, right down to the individual pores on your skin as you sit in the wheelchair waiting to be tested. I see every single dark strand of hair sticking up out of your scalp."

Alphie rubbed a hand self-consciously over her skull, but she couldn't help smiling, enjoying his description of her. Perhaps he watched her as much as she watched him. "I mean, do you ever see things that aren't really there. Like . . . just before the pain hit me today, I thought I saw a bright flash, and these glowing lights hovering in the air."

Beta was silent for a moment, and Alphie hoped that he was just thinking, rather than assessing her level of crazy. "Sometimes, when Miss Carmen takes me outside to be tested, the sun is so bright that I see spots all over the place. Maybe it was like that—was there a bright lightbulb in your Examination Room?"

Alphie shook her head and then realised that the gesture was pointless. "No, it wasn't like that. There was nothing there . . . and then there was."

"What do you think it was?"

Alphie thought for a moment. "Do you remember in Cinderella, how she had a fairy godmother?"

"You have *got* to be kidding me." It was Delta's voice, and it wasn't kind.

"Oh, so now you feel like talking to us," said Alphie, huffing.

"There's nothing much else to do," complained Delta-21.

"Well, I wasn't talking to *you*."

"It doesn't matter if you were talking to me or not, I could hear you so I'm going to reply. No, you didn't see your bloody fairy godmother. There's no such thing."

"You don't know that," said Alphie, trying to block out the giggle from one of the other cells.

"Yes, I do," said Delta-21, voice rising. "If it was anything, it was more likely a ghost—the ghost of a prototype who died down here from being bored and listening to people mutter about stupid fairy tales."

Goosebumps rippled along Alphie's arms as she rolled over. "It wasn't a ghost. Nobody dies down here, silly—they get tested, and then they join GenoCorp, just like Delta-20."

"Actually," said Zeta-7, and Alphie's stomach plummeted, "I heard Miss Carmen and Scott talking about Delta-20. She didn't go to GenoCorp."

"What do you mean?" asked Epsilon. "Where did she go?"

"She was retired," said Zeta-7.

"Retired?" repeated Alphie, trying to recall if she had ever heard of such a thing as prototypes being retired. "What does that mean?"

"I don't know. They didn't say any more. Miss Carmen seemed mad, though."

Alphie stared up at the ceiling, mulling this new information over in her brain. It made her head hurt even more.

"You should ask her about it, Alphie," said Zeta. "Miss Carmen likes you better than all of us."

"That's not true—"

"Aww Alphie," said Beta-6, "sure it is. Or at the very least, she's less scared of you than the rest of us."

That part was true. "Okay," said Alphie, rubbing a hand over her scalp. "I'll do my best."

"So what's the deal with you?" asked Delta-21. "Alphie?"

"The deal?"

"You were saying earlier that our DNA is *enhanced*. Like we have some sort of abilities. I don't suppose you can bend these bars and get me out of here?"

I wish, thought Alphie. "Nope," she said aloud. "I can just decode stuff. Letters, numbers . . . patterns. That sort of thing."

"How useful," said Delta, her voice filled with sarcasm. A soft thud came from Delta's cell, as though she had thrown herself down on the bed.

"That's why we are in a low-security zone," explained Alphie. "All the really useful modifications—the ones that could be dangerous—those prototypes are kept somewhere else. Zeta can hear them talking now and then, when the doors are open at just the right time."

"Interesting," said Delta-21, but her voice sounded bored. "And you, to my right . . . Gamma? What's up with you?"

"I'm impervious to poison," said the wispy voice. "Well, mostly . . ."

"Mostly?"

"I mean, some of the ones they give me make me really sick. There's nothing much I can do to help that—at least you guys can control your enhancements."

"It's not that I can really control my eyesight," said Beta, "just with practice it gets better. I'm Beta, by the way—I can see really far, and in the dark too." Alphie thought she could detect a note of pride in his voice. He had always liked Delta-20 . . . was he going to be the same with Delta-21? A pang of jealousy rocked Alphie's body and she tried to ignore it.

"I can hear a finger tapping on a table a kilometre away . . . well, except through soundproof walls," said Zeta from the furthest cell.

"What about you?" asked Delta. "Boy in the cell next to me. Epsilon?"

"If I concentrate really hard, I can't feel pain."

"None at all?" asked Delta, voice filled with curiosity. She seemed to be coping with her newfound circumstances in Zone One a bit better now. "Like . . . what if they cut your foot off?"

"They've cut three fingers off so far, and I only felt one of them. That was before I learnt how to really block it out."

Delta whistled. "Uh-huh, okay."

Alphie thought back to when she had first woken up in Zone One, so long ago. "Other than learning to use our enhancements," she said, "the strangest thing to get over is having no memories."

"What do you mean?" asked Delta.

"Like, this is day one, today, like you've just been born. Miss Carmen told me that they play us videos and things while we are being created so we know how to speak."

There was silence from Cell 4.

"So . . . what's my enhancement?"

"Shhh," said Zeta-7, "he's coming back."

A moment later, the door clicked open and Scott re-entered the zone, taking up position near the end of the corridor.

CHAPTER 8

Peering through the bars of Cell Four, Carmen's gaze swept from one side of the small room to the other. The setup was the same as all the other cells in Zone One—a low lying bed, a toilet and sink in the back, and nothing much else. Sometimes she wondered if AWPA should give them more. Something to distract them between the tests, perhaps. But Lucinda had assured her this was all the prototypes needed.

"Delta-21," said Carmen, "assessment time." She made sure that her feet were placed firmly on the far side of the yellow line.

The new prototype slowly pulled back the thin blanket and glared up at her from the bed. Its white-blonde hair created a stark contrast with its dark skin and eyes. *Was that natural,* wondered Carmen, *or a result of its enhancements?* Either way, it was in serious need of a haircut.

"Scott, make sure the prototype gets cleaned up this weekend," she said to the older guard. Then she glanced over the other prototypes in Zone One, noting their ragged appearances. "Make sure they all do. Soap. Shaved heads. The works."

"No problem," said Scott.

Carmen turned back to the prototype lying in the cell in front of her. "Delta-21, it's the middle of the day," she said in a disapproving voice. "You can't lie around in bed all day." Carmen could see a plastic tray of food lying untouched on the floor of the cell and sighed. If the prototype didn't eat, then it wouldn't have the energy to use its enhancements "Scott, a little help, please."

The guard appeared at her side with the control for the stun-band gripped in his hand. "You've seen one of these?" he asked the prototype, and it gave a small nod. "Then I suggest you get your act together quickly."

The prototype rolled forward and stretched its legs out, placing its bare feet on the cold concrete floor as though it was unstable.

"Do you think it's all right?" asked Carmen under her breath, and Scott shrugged.

"The Delta models have always been a bit hit-or-miss."

Delta-21 stood up and moved closer, peering through the bars at Carmen. Beneath the orange clothes, its skin was dark as night, and its blonde hair fell to its waist in straggly knots. It crossed its arms across its chest and looked at her uncertainly.

"Hello," said Carmen, slowly, wondering how much understanding this one had. The notes from the mainland facility were fairly sparse, but they did hint at the high hopes they had for this prototype.

"Hello," said the prototype, mimicking Carmen's style of speech. It was a little unnerving.

"Scott," said Carmen, stepping back so the guard could do the required checks.

"Wrists," he said, and the prototype held its hands out towards him. "Closer, closer—I'm not going to bite."

Delta-21 stepped right up to the bars and Scott scanned the tattoo on its wrist. It seemed jumpy, as if it thought something bad was going to happen at any moment.

"Turn around," said Scott, but the prototype just looked at him.

"Why?"

Scott laughed, but not unkindly. Carmen enjoyed working with Scott—unlike Michael, he did seem to understand that however unnatural the prototypes were, they still had genuine thoughts and feelings. "Try that with any other guard and you'd have a few thousand volts of electricity running through your body. First rule in Zone One—don't talk back. Don't ask questions. Turn."

The prototype narrowed its eyes but complied, shifting so that Scott could check the settings on the stun-band around its neck. Scott inserted a small tool into the back of the device and tightened the band.

"Good to go," said Scott, and Carmen retrieved the wheelchair from behind the door to the examination rooms. "When I open your cell," said Scott, slowly, in case the prototype had any trouble understanding, "you need to walk directly over to the wheelchair and sit down. Got it? No funny business, or you'll drop so fast you won't know what hit you." The guard flashed the small regulator at the prototype, and Delta-21 nodded to show that it understood.

Carmen stepped behind Scott and watched as he opened the door and the prototype moved compliantly across to the wheelchair.

"Put your arms and legs into the slots and press down firmly," said Scott.

The prototype jumped as the bonds clamped tightly around its limbs.

Scott leaned in towards Carmen. "It seems a bit jumpy," he said under his breath. "I need to do one more sweep of Zones Three and Four, then I can join you for the duration of the tests. Just wait here for a few minutes, if you aren't comfortable taking it through to the Examination Rooms alone."

Carmen hesitated for a moment, weighing up her options. "It's okay," she said at last, "I'll get it started. I'll be in Room Three when you're ready." She pulled the regulator from her belt and deactivated the location restrictor on the prototype's stun-band. Then she pushed the wheelchair carefully along the corridor. As she moved through the door at the end, Carmen kept her gaze turned away from the small prototype peering through the bars in the final cell. She didn't need any distractions this afternoon.

***

Examination Room Three was split perfectly down the middle by a clear piece of plexi-glass. Carmen wheeled Delta-21 into one half of the room—the observation area—disengaged the locks on the wheelchair, and then retreated to the other side of the glass, keeping the stun-band regulator gripped in her hand at all times.

With the door firmly locked between them, Carmen sat down at the desk and spoke into the microphone mounted on the corner. "Okay, Delta-21. You may stand up and remove your clothes."

Carmen logged onto her laptop and downloaded a file from the sharepoint marked *Delta.Test1*. When she looked up again, the prototype was standing against the glass, staring in at her. It was still fully clothed.

"Delta-21," said Carmen, turning the microphone up in case it couldn't hear her, "your enhancements can only be tested properly if you are naked. Please remove your clothes and place them on the wheelchair."

The prototype raised an eyebrow and Carmen had the feeling that it was staring straight into her skull, penetrating her brain. There was a light knock on the door, and Carmen welcomed the distraction from the prototype's intense gaze.

"How's it going so far?" asked Scott, as he entered the room.

Carmen shrugged. "We'll get there."

The prototype was still standing near the plexi-glass, arms crossed over its body.

"We can do this the easy way or the hard way, Delta-21." Carmen held the regulator in the air, and this finally sparked the prototype into action, removing its loose orange clothes and draping them over the wheelchair. It unsuccessfully tried to cover itself with its arms. "It'll lose its modesty soon enough," Carmen murmured to Scott.

She connected the laptop wirelessly to the screen behind the prototype. "Okay, Delta-21, welcome to AWPA, the Advanced Weaponised Projects Agency. You are a genetically altered prototype, and your job is to do everything that I say."

The prototype raised an eyebrow, but it didn't say anything.

"There is one possible way out of here, and that is to meet—or surpass—your genetic potential. Impress the people in GenoCorp and you can join the big boys and girls on the outside."

"Doing what?" asked Delta-21.

"Whatever they want you to do," said Carmen.

The prototype ran its fingers through the ends of its long, white hair, tugging on the knots. "And if I don't manage to *surpass my genetic potential*? What happens then?"

"You will," said Carmen, "don't worry."

"And if I don't?" The prototype's face was drawn, a frown furrowing its brow.

"Delta-21," warned Scott, holding up the stun-band regulator.

"It's okay," said Carmen, "I don't mind answering its questions. It might help to motivate it to succeed." She leaned towards the microphone. "You stay here at AWPA until you reach your potential," she said. "Understand? The harder you work, the sooner you get to leave."

The prototype narrowed its eyes, but it didn't say anything else.

"Now, take a look at the screen behind you. In a moment, it will show a colour. Your job is to alter the pigment in your skin so that you blend in with that colour. Got it?"

The prototype cocked its head to the side.

"Scott, would you mind turning on the video cameras?"

Scott nodded and walked over to a box mounted on the wall, opened the door, and pressed a button. At the same time, Carmen activated the test file, and the large screen dominating the wall behind the prototype flickered to life, displaying a warm brown hue.

Delta-21 stared at the screen for a moment, then turned back towards Carmen. "I don't understand."

"The ability to change your skin colour is a part of your DNA."

"What, like a chameleon?"

"Actually, your particular enhancements come from the Mimic Octopus," said Carmen, "but it's the same principle. The ability is there, contained within you—you just need to work out how to activate it. Concentrate, Delta-21, on the colour behind you."

The prototype turned towards the screen and studied the colour in front of it. Carmen watched intently, looking for even the slightest hint of a colour change anywhere on the prototype's body. Leaning over, she turned the dial on the regulator to the lowest voltage and pressed the button that would administer a small shock through the prototype's stun-band.

"Ouch," said Delta-21, its hands flying up to the dark band encircling its neck. It turned towards Carmen. "What was that for?"

"Pain can help to kick-start the process," explained Carmen, turning the dial up and pressing the button again.

The prototype jumped and narrowed its eyes so that Carmen could feel the hatred radiating through the plexi-glass.

"Your body reacts to the pain in any number of ways," continued Carmen. "Fight or flight are both impossible in your current surroundings. What we want is a third response. Change."

Delta-21 turned towards the screen, concentrating on the colour before it.

"How far do you think this one will go?" asked Scott, peering through the glass with interest.

"It's too early to say," said Carmen, as the screen transitioned from brown to teal. She leaned towards the microphone. "How about this one, Delta-21. Concentrate."

"I am concentrating," said the prototype, hands balled into fists.

Carmen pressed the button on the regulator again and gave it a small zap. The prototype whirled around and faced her, eyes blazing with the exact colour of the screen.

"Very good," said Carmen lightly, "let's try another one."

***

By the end of the first hour, the prototype's eye colour was changing to match each slide without too much encouragement.

Halfway through the second, the skin on its left wrist was shifting too.

"Maybe it's a bit more sensitive there," said Carmen to Scott, "because of the tattoo?"

The guard shrugged. "Maybe. Can we wind this up soon?" he asked, glancing at his watch. "I don't mean to be pushy, but it's technically my lunch break."

"Oh, sorry Scott, this'll be the last one." Carmen flicked over to the next screen. "Final slide, Delta-20," she said, leaning towards the microphone. "Let's see if we can make some real progress before we stop for lunch."

After a few minutes of trying—punctuated with some well-timed zaps from the stun-band—Carmen was pleased to see that the prototype's irises and entire left arm had adopted an azure hue.

"Very good," said Carmen.

The prototype turned towards her, an unreadable expression on its face. "I don't want to be here," it said.

"That's fine," said Carmen, closing down the testing program. "You've made enough progress for today. We'll pick back up from here tomorrow."

"No," said Delta-21, its hands visibly shaking, "I don't want to be in my cell either. I don't want to be at AWPA."

"I'm afraid that you don't have much of a choice."

The prototype gave a strangled cry and rubbed a hand over its face. "I just want to go home."

Carmen shook her head, caught between amusement and frustration. "This is your home, Delta-21. The only one you have."

CHAPTER 9

Alphie's head still ached when Delta-21 was wheeled back into Zone One. The smell of the food in the plastic tray on the floor was nauseating, and she desperately wanted to go back to sleep.

As the prototype was taken past her cell, Alphie raised her head slightly to see what condition Delta was in. The prototype's eyes were fully black, so she had clearly gained some control of her abilities. Of course she had—the Delta models never stayed at AWPA for long.

Alphie tried to push the bitter thought away, but it was difficult when she hadn't even been able to finish the morning assessment. Part of her wanted to beg Miss Carmen to test her again, but the pain in her head and the heaviness in her limbs told Alphie that she was in no condition for assessments right now. She hoped that she wasn't getting sick.

"Delta, how did you go?" asked Epsilon-10, once the guard had left the area.

Alpha-3 couldn't make out the mumbled words coming from Delta's cell, but Zeta's laughter raised goosebumps on her forearms.

"What did she say?" asked Alphie, tracing a finger over the rough weave of the blanket.

"She said she's going to kill everyone here."

A couple of prototypes laughed, and there was a snort from the cell next to Alphie.

"Good luck with that," said Beta-6.

"Well, why else are we here?" asked Delta-21. "What's our purpose?"

"Not to try to kill the people who have control over our very existence," said Beta-6, but Alphie could hear the smile in his voice. He admired Delta-21 and her fearlessness. Alphie just thought she was being stupid.

"To pass all the tests," said Alpha-3, practically, "and reach our genetic potential. That's our purpose."

"And then what?"

"We join GenoCorp."

Delta laughed unkindly. "And then whoever they are—this so called *GenoCorp*—has control over us. No thanks."

"Then you'll be stuck here forever," said Alpha-3, pulling the blanket all the way up to her chin. "Is that what you want?"

"Maybe I won't be," said Delta-21. "Maybe I'll be retired instead."

"We don't even know what that is," said Beta-6. "I don't think you should bank on an alternative when you don't even know what it means."

"I asked Miss Carmen about it."

"Really?" said Alphie, sitting up in her bed. "What did she say?"

"I asked her what would happen if I couldn't pass the tests. She said I'd stay at AWPA until I reached my full potential."

"Exactly," said Alphie, "and that's what we've always been told. Maybe Zeta heard wrong—"

There was an uproar at Alphie's statement.

"I'm just saying," said Alphie, speaking louder so that she could be heard over the other prototypes, "we've never heard of 'retirement' until now. We've always been told that we stay until GenoCorp takes us."

"Whatever retirement is," said Delta-21, "it's got to be better than being here, or being bossed around by GenoCorp."

"So you're not even going to try?" asked Gamma, sounding shocked. "You're just going to do nothing until they retire you?"

"Yep," said Delta.

"You don't want to fulfil your potential?"

"Not for some woman who thinks it's fun to hurt me."

Alphie rubbed the fibres of the blanket between her fingers, creating static electricity. "Miss Carmen doesn't enjoy hurting you," she said. "She's just doing it to help you learn to control your enhancements."

Delta wasn't the only one who laughed at Alphie's statement.

"It's true," said Alphie, indignantly. "Miss Carmen—"

"Miss Carmen is a liar," said Delta-21. "She gets a thrill out of making us suffer."

"That's not true," said Alpha-3, her voice rising along with her emotions. "You only just got here, you don't even know her."

"Oh, and you do?"

"Yes," said Alphie. "I've been here longer than any of you. I know that she just wants us to succeed."

Even Beta-6 laughed at her, and Alphie shrank down on her bed, punching the thin mattress.

"She might be nice to you for whatever reason," said Beta-6 gently, "but for most of us, the assessments could be a lot less painful."

Alphie rolled onto her back, staring up at the ceiling. "Do you want me to tell you a story?" she asked, changing the subject.

"No," said Delta-21, "I'm not a baby like you. I don't need fairy stories to tell me that everything's going to be all right. I know it won't be."

Alpha-3 gritted her teeth, hoping that Beta would stand up for her. Nothing.

"But one thing I don't understand," said Delta-21 slowly, "is why? What are we to them? To this *GenoCorp*?"

"Weapons," said Gamma, her voice high-pitched and wispy. "Or at least prototypes of weapons."

"Gamma's right," said Zeta. "I've caught whispers over the years, and I've done my best to piece them together. From what I understand, someone—or a few someones—pay a lot of money to keep this place open. The idea is that we will be a new breed of soldier, or secret services operative, or something like that."

"What do you mean?" asked Delta.

"We look like normal humans, right?" said Zeta. "You can't tell that there's anything different just from looking at us."

"I guess . . ." said Delta.

"But humans can't hear someone's heartbeat from half a kilometre away. I can. Imagine a soldier who could pinpoint exactly where the enemy was hiding by the whoosh of blood in their veins. Or a spy who could clearly hear a conversation from the other side of a building."

"But why lock us up?" asked Delta. "Shouldn't we be kept in some fancy resort living in luxury if we are so important to them?"

"It's because they are scared of us," explained Gamma. "In here, kept behind bars with a disabler attached to our necks, they feel safer."

"Well I want to leave," said Delta-21.

"And go where?" asked Epsilon. "We're not human. Not really. Nobody would accept us in the outside world. Nobody except GenoCorp."

"That's what you say," said Delta. "*I* think they're lying to us."

"In what way?"

The sound of Delta running her hands along the bars with a musical clang echoed around Zone One. "You said you can't remember life before AWPA. Well, I do remember something."

There was silence as this statement sunk in.

"Do you remember being created?" asked Beta.

"No," said Delta. "I remember water."

"Like a tank?" prompted Beta. "A tank of liquid that you were grown in?"

"No," said Delta, voice firmer this time. "It wasn't a tank. It was a river. I remember a big river flowing through a city."

"Maybe you were dreaming," said Gamma. "I've dreamt about stuff like that sometimes too."

"How could I dream it if I've never seen it?" asked Delta, her voice rising. "If we're created in tanks then how do I even know what a river is? How do you?"

"The videos—" began Alphie.

"Bullshit."

"Shh," warned Zeta-7, clanging her hands against the bars.

A moment later the door clicked open and their conversation was put on hold as Scott re-entered the room. Alphie didn't mind—the discussion was making her far too uncomfortable anyway. Delta-21 was just like Delta-20 and Delta-19—a troublemaker intent on destroying the relative calm in Zone One. Lying back on her bed, Alphie couldn't help sighing, thinking that if history was anything to go by, at least Delta-21 wouldn't be around for long.

CHAPTER 10

Alphie walked in slow rectangles around the exercise yard, keeping one hand against the concrete perimeter. Her breath made white clouds in front of her, thick in the cool early-morning air.

The other prototypes walked or ran around the small area, enjoying the feel of the sun on their cheeks—even if it wasn't strong enough to warm them up. Gamma lay in the centre of the yard, staring up at the rectangular patch of sky above her. Alphie gazed upwards as well, hungrily taking in the small snippet of the outside world as she walked. One day. One day.

Delta approached Alphie as she reached the furthest corner of the yard.

"What do you want?" asked Alphie, still annoyed at the previous afternoon's conversation.

"I just want to chat," said Delta, and Alphie noticed that her eye colour had shifted to a faded grey. "Alphie, how good did the other Deltas get?"

"What do you mean?" asked Alphie, leaning against the cool bricks. "Good enough to join GenoCorp, clearly. None of the other prototype lines is up to twenty-one, if you hadn't noticed."

"Or bad enough to be retired," said Delta-21, and Alphie rolled her eyes. "Look, I just want to know how well they could alter their appearance." Delta leant against the wall, mimicking Alphie's stance. "Professor Rhodes wanted me to blend in with plain colours, and I couldn't do it. Not yet, anyway."

"You'll get there," said Alphie, trying to put her personal opinions aside and be encouraging. "I saw your eyes when you came back yesterday—they had changed."

"I don't need your encouragement."

Delta's sneer pierced through Alphie, and she pushed herself off the wall, continuing wandering around the rectangular space. If Delta couldn't be civil to her, then she wasn't going to go out of her way to answer her questions.

Delta-21 followed closely behind Alpha-3. "I just need to know how good they managed to get. Was it only plain colours that the other Deltas managed to change into, or more complex environments? How did they manage to do it? I mean, could I eventually blend into this brick wall?"

"I dunno," said Alphie, turning to face her. "I'm not a Delta."

The other prototype raised an eyebrow. "No need to be so touchy, I was just asking questions."

"Well, don't," said Alphie, stalking off to join Beta-6 who was lifting Epsilon above his head and turning in circles. Pale bandages stuck out from beneath Epsilon's orange clothes, and the one on his hand was spotted with blood.

"Proximity warning," blared Scott's voice from a speaker on the wall. "Beta-6, put Epsilon down."

Laughing, Beta placed the prototype back on the ground and turned to Alphie.

Noticing the look on her face, he sat down on the stairs and patted the step beside him.

"You shouldn't let Delta get to you so much," he said, as Alphie sat down.

"She doesn't," retorted Alphie, and Beta gave her a look. "Okay, she just gets on my nerves, okay. They all do. Every single Delta."

"Maybe it's because they are always gone so quickly, never hanging around for long."

"Maybe," said Alphie, watching as Epsilon engaged in an earnest conversation with the blonde-haired prototype. Delta-21 was gesturing towards his bandaged hand, saying something that Alphie couldn't hear. It was strange to see a prototype with hair—everyone else had been bald for so long, that it was hard to remember their original hair colour. Except for Beta-6, with the golden stubble gracing his scalp.

"She's so new, still trying to come to terms with her existence here. Try to cut her some slack."

Alphie sighed, resting her head against Beta's shoulder and closing her eyes. A light breeze played across her face, and Alphie was certain that she could smell the sea. If she stayed perfectly still, she could almost—almost—trick herself into believing that she was somewhere else.

"Proximity warning," blared the speakers again, interrupting her reverie. "Alpha-3, move away from Beta-6 or suffer the consequences."

Alphie stood up, stretching, as a regular beeping sound echoed around the exercise yard.

"Alright, Zone One prototypes, you know the drill." Scott's voice boomed from the speakers. "Up, up, up!" said Scott. "Out where I can see you."

Alphie joined the other prototypes in the centre of the exercise yard where the eye-like monitors could get a clear view of them all.

The speakers crackled, and then Scott's voice was replaced with the familiar recording of a woman barking orders at them. Alphie started jogging on the spot, only half-listening to the directions shouted at them through the speaker.

"Running on the spot. One, two, three, four. Knees higher. Feel the burn."

Feel the burn indeed. It was the same recording every week, so Alphie knew it off by heart.

"Time for push-ups. On the ground. Now. Ready, and—"

The recording cut in and out, which made it more amusing than usual. "Push . . . in the right . . ." Maybe the wiring had finally started to wear out. Perhaps there were rats in the walls that had nibbled on the backs of the speakers. It didn't really matter—the prototypes had been following the same instructions each week, so they knew the drill. All except for

Delta, who huffed and complained loudly, before receiving a zap through the stun-band.

"Sit-ups are a great way to tone those abs," announced the bodiless voice, and Alphie smiled—it was her favourite part of the recording and each week she listened out for it. It was the one statement that seemed so far removed from everything they were doing here—why would prototypes care about toned abs? It made her think that the recording was originally created for something else, and had simply been borrowed by AWPA. She liked to imagine women on the outside following the exercise routine from the comfort of their houses overlooking the ocean.

As the prototypes continued their exercises, Scott re-entered the yard from a door at the top of the steps, accompanied by a woman also wearing a black guard uniform. Alphie hadn't seen her before—she was young, and she looked nervously around at the prototypes. Scott said something to her and she disappeared back through the door, appearing a moment later with a small stool and a box clasped under her arm.

As the voice from the speaker faded away, Scott gestured for the prototypes to line up along the back wall of the exercise yard. Alphie rubbed a hand through the stubble on the top of her head as she took her place beside Delta-21, watching the guard place the stool in the centre of the yard, with the box beside it.

The nervous guard gripped her stun-band regulator as Scott walked down the line, snapping handcuffs around the wrists of each prototype. "Delta, you're up first."

"For what?"

"A haircut."

"I don't want one."

"Nikki?" Scott nodded at the new guard and a moment later Delta-21's hands flew to her neck with a grunt. Her eyes blazing with hatred, Delta-21 followed Scott to the centre of the yard and sat on the stool.

Retrieving some hair clippers from the box beside the chair, Scott began to shave the prototype's head, the white-blonde locks falling to the ground along with the tears streaming down Delta's face.

CHAPTER 11

Alpha-3 grimaced and tilted its head back against the wheelchair.

"Again?" asked Carmen, pausing the flow of data on the screen. "*Another* headache? Jesus Christ, that's the fourth in as many days."

Alpha-3 nodded, tears welling up in its eyes. "I'm sorry, Miss, I don't know what's going on. Maybe it's the screens."

"We tried going back to paper yesterday," Carmen reminded the prototype, "and you still said it was painful."

"Did the results come back from the scan?"

"Mmmhmm," said Carmen, "nothing showed up. We can't keep stopping partway through an assessment. For today, you're just going to have to push through it. Understand? That's the only way to join GenoCorp."

A tear rolled down the prototype's cheek, but it nodded, trying—and failing—to tilt its head against its bonds to rub the tear onto the orange material of its shirt. "I'm trying hard, I promise."

"I know, Alpha-3." Carmen sighed and ran a hand through her hair. Friday. Saturday. Sunday. Monday. Each day, the prototype had suffered from migraines early in the assessment procedures. Lucinda wouldn't be happy. She would want Carmen to push the prototype further and further until its true potential could be mapped. Lucinda would tell her to keep going until the prototype snapped.

"Again," said Carmen, but the prototype shook its head, crying harder. Now, clear snot was starting to trail down its face and Carmen recoiled with revulsion. No, this wouldn't do—she wouldn't get anywhere using her current tactics.

Turning off the video cameras, Carmen took a tissue out of the pack in her bag and gently wiped the prototype's eyes and encouraged it to blow its nose. Slowly, Alpha-3's sobs quietened to gentle sniffs.

"What will happen to me," asked Alpha-3, "if I can't reach my genetic potential?"

This again. "You'll stay here until you do," said Carmen, "so you just have to try harder."

Alpha-3 looked up at her with wide, dark eyes. "Are the cameras off?" the prototype asked.

"Yes," said Carmen, "why?"

"Because I know about Delta-20."

Carmen was silent, tapping her finger on the desk. "What exactly do you think you know about Delta-20," she said slowly.

"I know that she was retired."

Carmen looked closely at the prototype's face, wondering how the hell it knew about Delta-20, and more importantly, what she should do with this information.

"You're right," said Carmen at last, "Delta-20 was retired."

Alpha-3 seemed to deflate in front of her, and Carmen cursed herself—the prototype hadn't been one hundred per cent sure after all. But it had clearly heard something, somewhere. "How many of the other prototypes are aware of this fact?"

"All of them," said Alphie. "The thing is, we were wondering what it meant to be retired. Now that it seems that it might be my fate as well. It's nothing too bad, is it?" The prototype's bottom lip started to wobble again.

"Not at all," said Carmen, thinking quickly. "It just means that you're taken to a special facility on the mainland. You wouldn't have any friends there, or any clear purpose, so we wouldn't retire you unless we were absolutely certain that you couldn't reach your potential."

Alpha-3 thought about this for a moment. "Okay, Miss," it said, sniffing again.

"Listen, I've got something to show you," said Carmen, "something I brought back from the mainland." She reached into her bag and brought out the book, laying it on the table between them.

The cover was worn and faded, but Alpha-3 stared at it with wide eyes as though it was a relic in a museum. "The Little

Book of Fairy Tales," it said softly, reading the curly gold words sweeping across the front. Cartoon figures paraded across the cover of the book, marching along a leafy aisle.

Carmen lifted the cover, exposing felt-tip words scrawled on the inside. *This book is the property of Danielle Templeton.*

"This was my daughter's book," she explained to Alphie, "but she's too old for it now. I thought you might like to hear a story from it. And look at the pictures."

"How old is she?" asked Alpha-3.

"Seventeen."

Alpha-3 tapped one of her fingers on the arm of the wheelchair. "Why does your daughter have a different surname than you?"

"You ask a lot of questions," said Carmen. "Do you want me to read you a story or not?"

Alpha-3 nodded. "I do."

"Okay then," said Carmen, snapping the book shut, "let's get back to it. Show me what you can do."

The prototype looked disappointed, but then its expression turned to one of grim determination. Good.

Turning the camera back on, Carmen activated *Alpha.Test27* and the transparent screen attached to the wheelchair flickered to life.

CHAPTER 12

Alphie's eyes darted back and forth across the columns of text. Left, right, left, right. In her mind's eye, she saw the letters lifting off the screen and curling up into the air, then flying into her brain. Left, right, left, right. Alphie thought of her mind as being like a computer screen, similar to the one Miss Carmen had propped up on the table, except the information in Alphie's brain wasn't always filed away in pretty little folders.

"Keep going," said Miss Carmen.

Left, right, left . . . Alphie resolved to stuff as much information into her brain as possible, to input seemingly random data, sort through it, and work out the pattern. She was determined to please Miss Carmen, but even more so, she wanted to impress GenoCorp. The headache was still there, but if she could just ignore it, perhaps it would go away. Retirement didn't sound so bad after all, but having a purpose—joining GenoCorp—that was the ultimate goal.

A bright flash in the corner of the room distracted Alphie for a moment, and she glanced away from the screen.

"Concentrate," directed Miss Carmen, but Alphie's attention was drawn towards the shimmering pattern in the air behind the quality assurance assessor. It pulsed and shuddered as though it was alive. She wondered if she should be afraid or comforted by the strange apparition in the room.

"Look at the data, Alpha-3," said Miss Carmen. "Stop getting distracted."

If it was Alphie's guardian angel, it certainly looked nothing like she had imagined from the stories. But maybe she was wrong—if she could get Miss Carmen to read from the book of fairy tales, the pictures might give her more of an idea.

Suddenly, a searing pain exploded in Alphie's right temple and she screamed, leaning back in the wheelchair. "Miss—Miss Carmen," she said, back arching as far as it could against the clamps around her arms and legs. "Miss Carmen, it—it hurts!"

Alphie groaned, willing the pain to leave her as quickly as it had come, but instead, it just seemed to get more intense. Her nose tingled, and then a stream of crimson blood flowed down her chin and dripped onto her shirt.

She was dimly aware of Carmen pulling a radio out of her pocket and saying something through a crackle of static.

"Damn radio," said Carmen, jabbing at the button and then speaking into the transceiver again. "I need help in here. Examination Room Two."

Alphie's body contorted against the straps as she writhed with pain which moved from her head, down through her limbs.

"Calm down," said Carmen. "Breathe. The doctor will be right here."

The blood from her nose started to flow faster now, splattering down Alphie's orange shirt and onto her pants. "Miss . . . what's . . . happening?" Alphie's words escaped her lips between great panting breaths. The shimmering light was gone now, replaced by Miss Carmen's concerned face. Perhaps it hadn't even been real.

"I don't know," said Miss Carmen, looking desperately towards the door. "Deep breaths."

A fresh wave of pain hit Alphie and she cried out, closing her eyes against the agony that sent black spots careening into her vision. This was worse than the pain she had felt yesterday and the day before. She couldn't even feel the straps of the wheelchair anymore, or the edge of the stun-band as it cut into the skin around her neck. Even the walls of the examination room faded out of her awareness until it seemed like her entire existence was made up of pain. Just pain.

Alphie felt, rather than heard, someone else enter the room. She was dimly aware of a quick conversation between a man and Miss Carmen, and then there was a sharp prick in Alphie's upper arm.

For a minute or so, nothing happened—beads of sweat formed all over Alphie's body and she couldn't control the shaking that had taken over her limbs. Miss Carmen and the doctor stared at Alphie, until gradually she became more aware of her surroundings, and the pain ebbed to a dull ache. Relaxing back into the wheelchair, Alphie felt hot tears cascading down her face.

"I'm sorry, Miss Carmen." Her words sounded fragile as they flowed out of her mouth, as though any moment they would break into a thousand pieces.

"Has the pain gone?" asked Miss Carmen, as the doctor prised Alphie's eyelids open and shone the beam of his torch into her right eye.

"Uh-uh," said Alphie, her body increasing in heaviness as the medication took effect. "It's still there, but it's not so sharp now. More like a constant low-voltage surge from the stun-band rather than high-voltage shocks like before."

Carmen looked at the doctor with a worried expression on her face.

"Am I sick?" asked Alphie in a small voice. "Am I dying?"

The doctor didn't respond. Of course he didn't—prototypes didn't have the same rights as people, they didn't deserve answers.

"I don't want to die," said Alphie, trying not to cry. "I want to get out of here."

"Reactions are normal," the doctor said to Miss Carmen. "You're right to keep assessing."

Alphie felt her bottom lip wobble. "Right now?" she asked in a small voice. "Are we going to continue with the tests *right now*?"

"Thank you, Chris," said Miss Carmen. "That will be all." When the doctor left the room, she turned to Alphie with a sigh, wiping a tissue over the prototype's damp face. "No," she said at last. "No more tests today. I'll take you back to your cell and the guard can get you a fresh change of clothes."

Alphie sniffed, aware that her hands were still trembling with aftershocks from the pain. "What's happening to me, Miss Carmen?"

"I don't know, Alpha-3," replied the professor. "Blood tests and scans from yesterday came back normal. I honestly have no idea why you are reacting so violently to the tests. Could be the stress. You need to try to relax."

"Miss Carmen," said Alphie, remembering what she had seen moments before the migraine had hit her. "Just before the pain came, I saw something."

"What sort of something?"

Alphie's body gradually grew heavier, like the gravitational field had grown stronger just around her wheelchair. "Like a sort of light, hovering in the air behind you."

"Interesting," said Miss Carmen. "I'll let the medical staff know."

"I thought that maybe, maybe . . ." Alphie's eyes began to close. She felt tired and heavy, and the dull ache in her head was still there. She wanted to be sleeping beauty—to fall asleep and not wake up again for years and years.

"Maybe what, Alpha-3?"

As Alphie drifted out of consciousness, she thought that in her own fairy tale, it would be Beta-6 who eventually woke her up with a gentle kiss.

CHAPTER 13

From: <Rhodes.Carmen@awpa.mil>
To: <projectchrysalis@awpa.mil>
Attachments: 2

Subject: Prototype Alpha-3 Update

John,

As directed, Alpha-3's testing schedule has been increased, as has the quantity of information presented to the prototype.

I have some concerns about its reaction to these changes. It still has a human form, John, and there's only so much that a brain can hold before it snaps. In light of the most recent incident (see second attachment), I am requesting that the prototype be allowed a reprieve for the next week while we re-evaluate our approach.

I'm sorry to hear about you and Betty—I hope you're holding up okay.

Professor Carmen Rhodes

Reading over the email again, she deleted the second-to-last line, replaced it with a more professional, 'Regards,' and then clicked *send*. Then Carmen picked up her glass of red wine and swirled it around a couple of times before draining it in one gulp. Sighing, she rubbed her hands across her face, staring at the stained wine glass.

"May as well have one more," she murmured to herself, reaching across her desk for the wine bottle. Tipping it up, a few meagre drops of mahogany liquid slipped into her glass. "Damn."

Looking across at her bed, she contemplated crawling in between the covers—after all, it was nearly midnight—but sleep still seemed a long way off. Sending the email was supposed to make her feel better, and even if it didn't, the two glasses of red wine should have done something to cure her insomnia. Carmen massaged the tightness in her shoulders, staring at her glowing computer screen.

Minimising her emails, Carmen brought up the surveillance footage and focussed on Zone One, Cell One. A few minutes ago, the prototype had been sitting cross-legged in the centre of the small room. Now, it was lying on the ground.

Dead?

Carmen blinked a couple of times, peering into the infra-red monitor feed in a bid to work out whether the prototype was breathing. The surveillance feed flickered, and Carmen muttered under her breath about dodgy wiring as she waited for the image to reappear. After a moment of frustration, the picture became clear again, revealing the small body of the prototype splayed on the grey concrete floor. Its chest was rising and falling with the gentle intake of breath . . . maybe. Or was that just wishful thinking?

Reaching for the transceiver on the edge of her desk, Carmen decided to call the guard rostered on at the low-security zone and ask him to check on the prototype. Then she let her hand fall to her side. If the prototype was dead, then there was nothing much they could do about it until morning anyway. Besides, Michael was the current nightshift guard, and she didn't want to speak with Michael unless she absolutely had to. His method for checking if the prototype was alive would wake up the entire low-security zone with Alpha-3's screams.

Carmen closed the laptop lid and gazed for a moment at the little picture frame propped up against a pot plant on her desk. Two children—no, young adults, Carmen corrected herself— grinned out at her from behind the glass. Carmen tried to smile back.

"I'll be home soon, kiddos," she said quietly. Then she picked up the torch that was sitting beside the photo frame and stood up, pulling on her woollen jacket that had been draped over the back of the chair. It was still only Monday—she had another four days before she could go home. She definitely needed more wine.

Stepping out of her room and into the hallway, Carmen closed the door behind her, swiping her personnel card so that the door locked with a gentle beep. A plaque on the outside of the door announced that the room belonged to 'Professor Carmen Rhodes: Quality Assurance Assessor' in faded bronze. With all the downsizing that had been occurring, Carmen could have had a separate office to her living quarters now, but she'd chosen not to. The idea of having to move all of her folders to a new location made her tired just thinking about it. No, she was fine having her office located in the living quarters—after all, it reminded her of just how far down the hierarchy a quality assurance assessor in a low-security zone of AWPA really was.

Turning right, Carmen walked through the dimly lit corridor, her footsteps echoing slightly on the concrete floor. As she approached the end of the hallway, a security guard nodded at her, stepping aside. "Mrs Rhodes."

Carmen didn't bother correcting him. All women seemed to be 'Mrs' by default around here. Still, it would be nice if the staff would at least try to remember that she was no longer married. After all, it had been nearly a year since her split from Patrick.

Carmen put all thoughts of her ex-husband in a securely locked box, doused it with metaphorical petrol, and watched it burn as she went down two flights of stairs and entered the communal dining area. It was a big room which—during the day—was usually filled with scientists and doctors and off-duty guards. Ordinarily echoing with amiable chatter, right now the communal area was understandably deserted, silent, and filled with shadows instead of teeming with life.

Switching on the torch, the thin beam lit up the kitchen on the far side of the room—the light reflecting dimly off dull grey metal appliances. Carmen crossed the dining area and stepped behind the bain-marie, entering the main part of the kitchen. If it was daytime, the cooks would be ushering her back out of their territory, putting her back in her place on the other side of the bench. She smiled, opening the doors of the double fridge, and bent down to peer inside. *Beer. Beer. Beer. Aha, wine.* It was only a little bottle, but it would have to do.

Feeling thankful for the deep pockets in her jacket, Carmen dropped the bottle inside and moved back through the kitchen, planning on returning to her room and drinking herself to sleep. Halfway across the dining room, Carmen hesitated, training the torch beam onto the door to her right marked 'Secure Zone.' The large white letters glowed brightly in the otherwise dark room.

She shouldn't worry and yet . . . perhaps a little peek to confirm that the prototype was alive would settle her thoughts and help her to sleep. Before she could change her mind, Carmen walked briskly across the room and swiped her ID card through the scanner. The sealed door popped open with a high-pitched beep, admitting her inside.

***

The hallway leading to the secure zones was darker than the one outside Carmen's sleeping quarters. The dim lights interspersed evenly along the left-hand wall did little to illuminate the grey concrete floor or the doors leading off the corridor. Each door was marked with a single white digit, and Carmen hesitated on the threshold of Zone One, peering into the peephole mounted halfway up the door.

It was dark on the other side of the door, too, and she could just make out the corridor and the metal bars beyond. She couldn't see any guards in Zone One, so Michael must have been patrolling one of the other zones. Seizing the opportunity, Carmen took one of the stun-band regulators from its place on the wall, held it firmly in her hand, and then scanned her ID card against the door. The lock disengaged and Carmen stepped inside.

When the door closed behind her, she waited a moment for her eyes to adjust to the dimness of the area. She could have turned the lights up, but Carmen decided against it—if the prototypes were asleep, she didn't want to wake them, and she'd rather not alert too many people to her presence. She wanted to check on Alpha-3 and be out of Zone One before Michael came back and asked what she was doing.

It was the first time that Carmen had been inside Zone One during the night, and hearing the sounds of the prototypes breathing—without being able to see them—made the hairs on the backs of her arms prickle. She clutched the stun-band regulator tightly in her hand and stayed on her side of the yellow line.

Why was she here? To check on the prototype? There were doctors for that . . . but the doctors would all be asleep right now. She just wanted to know, one way or the other, if the prototype was alive. That way, maybe she could get some sleep.

Opposite Carmen, the space opened up to a series of dark cells. As she walked along the Zone One corridor, the sound of low snuffles and shuffles and whuffs emanated from the spaces to her right, but none of the prototypes spoke. Of course, they wouldn't speak after lights-out—they didn't want to get in trouble and suffer the consequences. Standard punishment was one zap at low voltage through the stun-band, but some of the guards—particularly Michael—were notorious for going overboard.

Carmen moved all the way to the end of the corridor—past the prototypes Zeta and Epsilon; past the new Delta; past Gamma and Beta—and stopped outside the final cell, the one closest to the examination rooms. A small sign with *Prototype Alpha-3* written in plain lettering was barely visible to the right of the bars. Carmen stood silently, holding her breath, trying to hear the low wheeze of the prototype breathing.

Silence.

Far out. She flicked the torch on, training it on the ground in the centre of the cell where she had last seen the prototype lying in the dull grey feed of the night-vision camera. The pool of light illuminated only bare concrete. Taking a deep breath, she edged across the yellow line and swung the torch to the right, towards the low bed pushed up against the wall.

"Hello, Miss Carmen."

Carmen gasped and stepped back, focusing her torch on the prototype standing to her left, close to the bars. If she reached out, she would be able to touch its bald head. Carmen's heart hammered in her chest.

"I'm sorry, Miss Carmen," whispered the prototype. "I didn't mean to scare you."

"You didn't," lied Carmen, ordering her heartbeat to return to a normal rhythm. "I just wasn't expecting you to be standing there, that's all. I was worried you were sick." Carmen much preferred it when the prototypes were safely strapped into their wheelchairs, unable to move.

On the other side of the bars, Alpha-3 squinted in the torchlight, its pupils reduced to tiny circles within its brown eyes. Carmen angled the beam downwards so as not to blind it.

"You were worried about me?" asked Alpha-3 with a small smile. "I'm fine, I just couldn't sleep, Miss."

Carmen frowned. "Do you still have a migraine?" She pictured Alpha-3 screaming in the middle of the examination, just a few hours earlier.

The prototype shook its head and Carmen relaxed a little. "No Miss, the headache went away soon after the docs gave me that jab." The prototype rubbed its hand absently over the thick, dark band around its neck. The dull metal of the stun-band seemed to consume all the light from Carmen's torch.

"That's good, Alpha-3," said Carmen. "How come you couldn't sleep then?" She kept her voice low, but Carmen had the unnerving feeling that the other prototypes were lying awake in their beds, listening to the hushed conversation.

Alpha-3 shrugged, its slight frame looking all the thinner for its slightly-too-large clothing. The faded orange shirt and pants gave the strange illusion that the prototype was a young, vulnerable girl, which, as Carmen knew, was far from the case. It should get easier, after all these years, to maintain a sense of objectivity, but for some reason, it seemed to get harder instead. Carmen realised with some annoyance that the prototype was still covered in blood—Michael hadn't given it a new outfit to get changed into as she had requested.

"I just had all these thoughts," explained Alpha-3, "running around in my head, crashing into one another. I'd tell one to be quiet and then a new one would pop up and they just kept going 'round and 'round and 'round." The prototype's wide eyes stared up at her, its pupils shrinking to pinpoints in the torchlight.

Carmen nodded. "I know what you mean."

"So even humans have information overload, huh?"

Carmen frowned. She knew what the prototype wanted to hear. "You are human, Alpha-3. You're just—"

"Different?"

"I was going to say *enhanced*."

"Same thing. Michael says I'm not human. He says I'm just the property of AWPA."

Carmen glanced down at Alphie's left wrist where the tattoo declaring her as a prototype belonging to AWPA was hidden in the shadows. "Well, you are," she said, "but that doesn't mean you're not human."

The prototype stepped closer to the bars, gesturing for Carmen to do the same. Carmen took a nervous half-step closer to the cell, positioning her finger over the appropriate button on the stun-band regulator, just in case. The prototype lowered its voice to barely a whisper. "Did you come here to read me a story from your book?"

"Shhh." Carmen ran the beam of her torch around the cell. If the prototype were to lie down on the ground, it would most likely be able to touch one wall with its toes and the other with its fingers. The cell was a little deeper than it was wide, but it was certainly no luxury hotel room. It didn't even have a window. "I said I'd read you one if you excelled in the test. If I remember correctly, you ended up being wheeled out by a medic."

The prototype at least had the decency to look abashed. "I'll do better tomorrow," it said.

The professor trained her torch back on the prototype, noting that its pale face was filled with determination. Did she really believe that the prototype was human? Nobody else seemed to. After all, it might have human parts and a human nervous system, but it definitely wasn't what you'd call normal.

"Actually, I've asked for you to have the rest of the week off. Take some time to recover, then back to it next week."

"Thanks, Miss." The prototype clutched the bottom of its baggy orange shirt, splattered with blood.

"All right, Alpha-3, it's time to get some rest."

The prototype nodded, a small smile on its face. "You can call me Alphie, you know," whispered the prototype. "Everyone else does."

Carmen was silent. "I don't think that's a good idea."

The expression on the prototype's face didn't change. "What do you do, Miss Carmen, when you can't sleep?"

Carmen could feel the solid weight of the wine bottle in her pocket and just about laughed. What indeed. "Sometimes I read," she said, under her breath.

The prototype made a face and raised one hand, holding the metal bar separating it from Carmen. Carmen resisted the urge to step backwards, instead gripping the regulator a little tighter. It would be hypocritical to care about whether Alpha-3 was breathing or not one minute, and then be scared of it the next.

"Well, that's not exactly an option for me. What else do you do to help you sleep, Miss?" the prototype whispered.

"Well, you could try counting sheep."

The prototype screwed up its nose. "I don't like sheep."

Carmen relaxed a little. The prototype wasn't going to die on her tonight. And perhaps tomorrow morning she would receive an email back from John telling her that she didn't need to push the prototype so far, that there would be some reprieve. And in just a few days, she would get to go home.

"It doesn't have to be a sheep," said Carmen. "You could imagine any animal you like. Horses. Butterflies. Or it doesn't even have to be an animal. You could imagine numbers floating overhead and count them instead. The whole idea is to focus on one thing so all the other information fades into the background."

Alpha-3 nodded. "It's been good talking to you, Miss, it made me forget a bit."

Forget what? Its headache? Or the fact that its entire existence involved being poked and tested and pushed to its very limits, all while living in a small, bare cell. "That's good,

Alpha-3. Now hop into bed and I'll check on you in the morning."

Carmen watched as the prototype crossed the cell towards its bed. "Oh, and Alpha-3?"

The prototype was immediately back against the bars, eager for any interaction. "Yes, Miss?"

"If the headache comes back—if it gets bad—you make sure you tell the guard, okay?"

The prototype nodded doubtfully.

Carmen wasn't convinced that the prototype would actually tell Michael if it was suffering. After all, the stun-band had trained it not to complain. She felt a little better, however, and as she moved back down the hallway, Carmen was hopeful that at last she would be able to get some sleep.

As she neared the end of the corridor, there was movement in the shadows and Carmen froze, her heart thumping in her chest. Visions of a prototype ripping her limb-from-limb swept through her mind as she held the stun-band regulator out in front of her.

"Who's there?" Her voice came out in a panicked squeak as she fumbled for her torch and switched it on.

The shadows were pushed back to reveal Michael standing near the door, his face impassive.

Carmen let out her breath. "Michael, far out you scared me. How long have you been standing there?"

"Long enough," said Michael, taking a step towards her. "What are you doing down here, Carmen?"

Carmen's legs felt like jelly as she lowered the beam of light. "There's no rule against me being here," she said, stepping around him to go out the door. "And by the way, you forgot to give Alpha-3 a clean outfit after the incident today."

His hand reached out like a vice to grip her upper arm.

Carmen froze, refusing to meet his eyes and reveal how much he intimidated her. "You're hurting me," she said quietly, trying to keep her voice steady.

"You shouldn't get so close to the prototypes," said the guard, his voice laced with ice. "You might give them hope."

"Thanks for the tip," said Carmen, trying to pull her arm out of his grasp. After a moment he let go, and she stumbled through the door, hands shaking all the way back to her room.

CHAPTER 14

Alpha-3 lay down on her bed and pulled the thin blanket up over her body. It could be cold in the cell sometimes, but she knew that she should count herself as one of the lucky ones. From the hushed whispers of the other prototypes, she gathered that those in higher-security zones had far less comfortable sleeping arrangements.

As she lay in bed with her eyes closed, willing sleep to arrive, Alphie wondered why Miss Carmen had come to check on her, really. For as long as she could remember, it had only been guards keeping an eye on her in the middle of the night. But Miss Carmen was clearly worried about the headaches and nosebleeds. Was Alphie really sick? The thought made goosebumps erupt along her arms and Alphie huddled down under the blanket even further. If she was sick, maybe she wouldn't be able to pass all of Miss Carmen's assessments. And if she didn't pass the tests, then . . .

Alphie pushed the thought away. The idea that she would be stuck in Zone One for the rest of her life, or retired to some isolated facility, caused a gaping hole to brew in her belly. It was like the time Michael refused to feed her for three days because she asked him if the prototypes who had joined GenoCorp would ever come back to visit. If she was sick, then the doctors had better figure it out quickly so that she could perform to the best of her ability.

Her mind wandered to Delta-21 and her insistence that she remembered a river from before her time at AWPA. What an attention seeker. It was tempting, of course, to make up stories about some past life that didn't really exist. To imagine some alternate future where they were proper humans and not prototypes at all. But Alphie knew better than that—*this* was reality, but she was happy to float away into the fairy tales that Miss Carmen told her, just the same.

Prototypes could be confusing creatures, thought Alphie . . . but so were humans. Some humans, like Miss Carmen, seemed to genuinely care about Alphie, to want her to do well in the tests, and to show concern when she was suffering. Miss Carmen would smile at her, and it would seem real, and she would do things like read stories to Alphie, which would probably get her into trouble if anyone found out.

But there were others, like Michael, who would say things like Alphie wasn't human, she wasn't really a girl—she was just the property of AWPA, the Advanced Weaponised Projects Agency. Alphie ran a finger over the small tattoo on her left wrist indicating that she certainly wasn't her own person. Created by AWPA, raised by AWPA . . . the only possibility of being anything other than a Zone One prototype was to join GenoCorp.

Sometimes Alphie wondered if she could be both; Prototype Alpha-3, genetic experiment, and Alphie, human teenager. If it wasn't so risky, she would have laughed aloud. From what she could tell, Alphie was about as far from a normal human teenager as someone could get. Normal teenagers had parents, for one thing. Pets. Boyfriends.

"Alphie."

The whisper echoed around her cell from the grate, and she hoped the guard hadn't heard. Crawling up onto her knees, Alphie put her ear against the grate in the concrete wall that let air flow between the cells.

"Alphie, are you still awake?"

Alpha-3 hesitated, listening for the familiar clonk of the guard's feet as he walked along the corridor to tell Beta to shut up, or pressed the button that would send a surge of electricity through the stun-band around his neck. There was no sound. "Yeah, I'm awake," she breathed.

"How are you feeling? Okay now?"

Alphie decided against sharing her fears with Beta-6.

"I'm fine. If I can have a few days off I'll be even better." Alphie leant against the bars of her cell and peered along the corridor.

"He's gone," said Beta-6. "Off patrolling somewhere else."

Alphie couldn't see very well, but she knew that she could trust Beta's eyesight.

"I asked Miss Carmen about retirement," she said slowly.

"Yeah? And?"

"It's a real thing," she said, stomach clenching uncomfortably, wondering if it was going to be her fate.

"Told you," came Zeta's voice from further along the corridor, but Alphie ignored her.

"And?" prompted Beta again. "What is it?"

Alphie rubbed her shoulder, working out the knots from her contortions in the wheelchair earlier. "Prototypes who aren't taken by GenoCorp are sent to some isolated facility on the mainland."

"That doesn't sound so bad," said Beta.

"Yeah, exactly. I'm sure Delta-20 will be happy. She might not have been accepted by GenoCorp, but at least there's no more tests."

CHAPTER 15

When Carmen woke up, a glowing 'message received' icon was waiting on her laptop in greeting. She took a deep breath and prepared to open the email, before the whole room lurched sideways and she scurried into the bathroom to empty her stomach.

When she was finally able to return to the bedroom, Carmen glared at the empty wine bottle on the desk. The room smelled of stale alcohol and the floor gently swayed from side-to-side.

"Pull yourself together, woman," muttered Carmen, tipping her water bottle up and draining it in a couple of gulps. Sliding a window open, Carmen closed her eyes as a cool sea breeze played across her face. Her headache receded a little, so she sat on her bed with her laptop and loaded her emails.

From: <projectchrysalis@awpa.mil>
To: <Rhodes.Carmen@awpa.mil>

cc: Greenwood.Lucinda@awpa.mil
Attachments: 0

Subject: Project Chrysalis Update

Good morning Professor,

Thank you for the update on Alpha-3. In the future, please remember to cc Lucinda into any requests such as these.

Carmen snorted and placed the laptop onto her bed, walking back into the bathroom to fill up her water bottle. There was a reason that she had asked John, the manager of Project Chrysalis, and not Lucinda, the head scientist, to take it easy on Alpha-3. Lucinda was a results-at-any-cost type of person, whereas John could be more easily swayed. Sometimes. The fact that John had so obviously cc'd the scientist into the email made her fingers twitch. Or perhaps that was just the wine.

Collapsing back onto the bed, Carmen took a deep breath before reading the rest of the email.

Lucinda and I met with the financial stakeholders last night. It didn't go well, I'm afraid. One of us will update you on the situation soon.

You are no doubt aware of what happened in low-security Zone Two. If we want to avoid something similar happening in Zone One, then we all need to knuckle down and produce exceptional results. I understand that you are concerned about Prototype

Alpha-3's welfare, and I'm sure these flags will be noted by Lucinda. In the interim, please continue with the tests as per normal.

I checked your schedule, and it appears that the next examination session for this particular prototype is at 11am this morning—I trust that you will continue to push the prototype to its full capacity.

Regards,

John Haven

Carmen gritted her teeth as she read the final few lines of the email. She considered calling John and talking some sense into the project manager. Then a fresh wave of nausea had her scurrying back to the bathroom—she was certainly not in any state to be making demands.

As Carmen dry-retched over the toilet bowl, she cursed the fact that she'd never been allowed to move up the ranks at AWPA. John had always made promises about moving her up to Zone Three or Four where the more *valuable* prototypes were kept, but they had proven to be empty words. Carmen had been stuck in Zone One for years, and now the not-so-subtle threat by mentioning the plight of Zone Two. Bastard.

Carmen peeled off her pyjamas and grabbed a fresh towel from the cupboard. Hopefully she could show some real progress today with Alpha-3, but if the last few days were anything to go by, she wasn't holding her breath.

She turned the shower on scalding hot, and as she waited for the water to heat up, Carmen thought about what John had said in his email. He was probably right, of course—Carmen shouldn't be so concerned about the prototype. After all, it was simply a test subject, a costly experiment that would be pushed to its limits and then either taken by GenoCorp or retired. Her concern over its welfare during the examination process was irrational—it had a clear purpose, and so did she.

However, the way that he always handballed issues onto Lucinda was irksome. *He* was the project manager, and he should bloody well grow a spine. And what was that about the meeting with the financial stakeholders? Surely they weren't considering closing down *another* zone.

Stepping under the blistering stream of water, Carmen tried to relax and let the wine leaching from her pores mingle with her concerns and flow down the drain.

***

Alpha-3 stared in horror at the dark red splatters soaking into the material on the legs of her pants.

"I'm—I'm sorry," she stammered, trying to reach a hand up to stem the flow of blood from her nose. The metal braces pinning her to the wheelchair cut into her wrists as the blood continued to stream down her chin and drip onto her lap.

On the opposite side of the table, Carmen sat hunched over her laptop. Through the thin screen attached to the side of the wheelchair, Alphie could see the woman typing away furiously, the wrinkles on her forehead more pronounced than usual as she concentrated on her task. Miss Carmen looked up now, gazed at the blood, and tut-tutted in exasperation. "Oh no."

Rising and moving around the table, Miss Carmen pushed the screen aside, clipping something firmly onto Alphie's nose to stop the bleeding. Then she grabbed a tissue, dabbing ineffectually at the splatters on Alphie's lap. The lines on the woman's forehead became even deeper.

"I'm sorry," repeated Alphie, the clip on her nose transforming her voice into a nasal whine.

"I know you do it just to get a clean outfit," said Miss Carmen, wiping a tissue over Alphie's chin.

"No," said Alphie, her stomach dropping, "I wouldn't do that. I can't control it. It just happens."

The quality assurance assessor gazed at Alphie, her eyes a dark blue that made Alphie think of the rectangle of sky she saw once a week from the exercise yard. "I was joking."

"Oh," said Alphie. An uncomfortable silence grew between them as Miss Carmen attempted to clean up the mess. "I suppose if I was human, I would have got that, huh?"

Miss Carmen swiped the tissue across Alphie's legs a couple more times. "Stop worrying so much about whether people think you're human or not, and focus on reaching your potential."

Alphie wiggled her nose as the clip pinched her skin. "I thought I was going to have the rest of the week off," said Alphie. "Time to recover. That's what you said."

"I tried."

"I guess you have to follow rules too, hey?"

Miss Carmen nodded at her. "Okay then, Alpha-3, let's keep going with the tests."

"Oh." Alphie glanced down at the blood on her clothes. "I just thought . . ."

"We have to keep going. We're only halfway through. Do you want to get out of here?" asked Miss Carmen.

Alphie frowned in confusion. "Like now, or forever?"

"Forever."

"Of course—"

"Because GenoCorp only takes the best."

"I know they only take the best," Alphie said dully. "I'm trying, I promise. It's just . . ." Alphie sighed, looking down at the blood drying on her orange pants.

"You have the potential to be the best, Alpha-3," said Miss Carmen gently, leaning forward across the table. "You just need to concentrate."

Alphie shrugged. "Did you bring the fairy tale book?"

"Oh, Alpha-3," said Miss Carmen, looking disappointed. "You know that's only if you do really well. It's for special occasions."

Alphie didn't say anything, worried that if she opened her mouth, she'd start to cry—and Miss Carmen didn't like it when she cried.

"Tell you what," said Miss Carmen, "you do well on this next test, and I'll read you a story tomorrow."

"Promise?"

"Have I ever broken my promises?" asked Miss Carmen.

Alphie shook her head. "Okay," she said, feeling her chest swell. "Let's do one more."

The woman beamed at her. "Good decision, Alpha-3."

Miss Carmen typed something into her laptop and then a series of letters and symbols appeared on the thin screen held a few inches in front of Alpha-3's face. "I want you to concentrate. Show me just what Alpha-3 can do."

Alphie took a deep breath and then focused on the letters transposed on the screen, shifting quickly from one set to the next. Her nose ached, but she tried to ignore it, concentrating only on the words in front of her. Relaxing her body and her mind, she watched the text flow down the screen in front of her, waiting for the usual patterns to reveal themselves.

Except that it didn't happen. Instead of the usual river of text shifting in an orderly fashion, the data was a jumbled mess of random digits swirling chaotically in front of her.

Alphie squinted her eyes, tilting her head slightly, willing the words to become clear as they usually did.

It was no use. "Uh, Miss Carmen?"

"Is there a problem?" asked the quality assurance assessor, pausing the program. The letters froze in their perpetual eddy, blurring slightly as Alphie peered through the words at Miss Carmen's concerned face.

"I can't read them," said Alphie, the realisation making her hand shake against the arm of the chair.

Miss Carmen leant forward, looking down at her laptop. "What do you mean you can't read them? It's similar to the data set we used just a few minutes ago."

"They don't make any sense," insisted Alphie, feeling the panic rising. "It's just squiggles and dots."

Miss Carmen stood up, walking around the table and readjusting the screen in front of Alphie.

"What about now?"

"Oh no," said Alphie, tears prickling in the corners of her eyes, "I'm going crazy like Epsilon-4, aren't I?"

"No," said Miss Carmen, "you're just tired. It's been a long day. We'll try again tomorrow." She closed the program down, causing the strange symbols to wink out of existence.

CHAPTER 16

"My office. Now."

Carmen looked up absently from the meal she was eating alone in the corner of the dining room to see Lucinda's retreating back already halfway across the room. "That's fine," Carmen muttered, "I wasn't hungry anyway." Leaving her tray for the cleaners to deal with, Carmen followed in Lucinda's wake, the older woman's dark bun laced with grey hairs bobbing up and down on the top of her head as she walked.

Lucinda always acted like she was on a mission, with little regard to niceties or stopping to smell the roses. And, to be fair, as head scientist of Project Chrysalis, she *was* always busy. It was Lucinda's job to oversee the prototypes from the moment they arrived at AWPA's examination facility. No wonder she always looked like she had a ruler up her—

"Sit." Lucinda unlocked her office door and directed Carmen towards one of the seats in front of a large, wooden desk piled high with neat stacks of paperwork.

Before sitting down, Carmen looked curiously around the woman's office, taking in the large oil painting on one wall, of a stern looking gentleman sitting behind a desk. She'd been at AWPA for several year, and this was the first time that Carmen had been summoned to Lucinda's office.

Lucinda followed her gaze to the portrait. "Rudolf Jaenisch, Professor of Biology at MIT. He was a pioneer of transgenic science, creating the first genetically modified animal in 1974." Lucinda sat down at the far side of the desk, plucking a file off the top of one of the piles.

"Was it a rat?" asked Carmen, feeling her skin crawl.

"Mouse," replied Lucinda. "By injecting retrovirus DNA into mouse embryos, he was able to integrate leukaemia DNA sequences into the mouse genome and show that these also transferred to its offspring."

So he gave a mouse cancer. What a hero, thought Carmen, but she didn't dare say it aloud. Instead, as she sat down, she just said, "Your inspiration, I assume?"

Lucinda looked up sharply as though checking if Carmen was mocking her.

Carmen kept her expression perfectly neutral.

"Yes, actually. I attended many of his lectures and followed his scientific progress almost religiously in my early years as a scientist."

"You think he'd approve, then, of what we are doing here at AWPA?"

Lucinda opened the file to the front document and perused the contents. "Absolutely."

Carmen looked at her watch. She still had one more prototype to test today. "What's this about, Lucinda? I'm scheduled to test Delta-21 in forty-five minutes."

"I know," said Lucinda, not looking up from the file, "I create the examination schedules."

Lucinda always had a way of making Carmen feel about ten centimetres tall.

"We're not here to talk about Beta-6. We're here to talk about Alpha-3."

"If this is about the stories—"

"Professor Rhodes, your assumption that I care about the methods you use to get results is insulting. However,"— Lucinda ran her finger down the page in front of her, perusing the text—"that's the problem, isn't it? You're not actually getting any results from Alpha-3."

"There have been some—"

"Issues. Yes, yes, I read your email. The thing is, Professor, we don't want prototypes with issues. We want prototypes who impress our financial stakeholders. Unfortunately, the only impressive thing about Alpha-3 right now is the amount of blood that can come out of its nose."

Carmen resisted the urge to bite back.

"You called off the assessment early today. And the day before. And"—Lucinda shuffled some paperwork in front of her—"the day before that. Care to explain?"

"The prototype was in pain, pushing it further wouldn't have achieved anything."

"That's not your decision to make," said Lucinda, her green eyes holding Carmen's gaze. "Your job is to deliver the assessments and to *motivate* the prototypes as required. It is *not* to decide whether to deliver the assessments or not."

"And if I push it too far? If the prototype suffers irreparable damage and has to be retired?"

Lucinda shrugged, leafing through the pages of data that Carmen had compiled over the past week. "That's just another form of data, isn't it? Just another piece of the puzzle."

"Yeah, an expensive piece," said Carmen.

"You're not the one paying the bills."

Carmen sighed, running a hand across her face. "Next week it'll do better," she said at last. "But it needs a rest, Lucinda. It needs time to recuperate."

"Perhaps," said Lucinda. "Or maybe this particular prototype has outstayed its welcome."

Carmen's heart thudded in her chest. "What? You're going to retire it like you did with Delta-20?"

The woman didn't say anything, continuing to peruse the data in the file.

"But it's improving," said Carmen, carefully. "Look at the data from last week. It's like something finally clicked in its brain and its decoding ability improved exponentially."

"Except," said Lucinda, snapping the file shut, "for the past few days."

"Right," said Carmen, "but the headaches could just be a short term thing. With a few days off, perhaps—"

"Do you really think so, Professor Rhodes? Or have you just become a little attached to this particular prototype."

"Of course not," said Carmen, shrinking under the gaze of both Lucinda and the oil painting on the wall. "I just think the prototype has more to offer."

"We'll see," said Lucinda, tapping her finger on the desk. "And what about the other prototypes? How are they going?"

Carmen raised an eyebrow, looking at the files in Lucinda's hands.

"Didn't you tell me that I couldn't just go off the data? That I should talk to you because *you know them best?* You can see potential where others might not . . . or some drivel like that?"

Carmen sighed. "Beta-6 has stopped improving," said Carmen. "It is simply maintaining its current optic levels—which are incredible, mind you, but I'm not sure that we are going to see advancements on the current achievement."

"Mmmhmm, and Gamma-11?" said Lucinda, writing something down.

"There are still some substances that Gamma reacts to, and I had to resuscitate it just a couple of weeks ago because it went into cardiac arrest. It hasn't reached its potential yet, and I think it will continue to impress us over time."

"And what about Delta-21?"

Carmen sat back in her seat. "It shows promise," she said with feeling. "It's still working on mastering single-colour transitions, but I doubt that it'll be long until we move onto more complex environments."

"Very well," said Lucinda, "you can return to your duties. Just be aware that if we don't show some decent results in Zone One, the stakeholders might withdraw their funding and it'll be a repeat of Zone Two."

"I understand," said Carmen, rising to her feet. "I'll keep you updated on my progress.

***

Carmen administered another shock through the stun-band and was pleased to see the skin on the prototype's abdomen rippling with waves of colour.

"Concentrate, Delta-21," she said into the microphone. "Once you can master single colours, we'll move onto more complex images."

It was a good way to end the day. She opened up the prototype's file and scrawled a few notes. Alpha-3 might be deteriorating, but Delta-21 certainly wasn't failing to impress. If the financial stakeholders were considering cutting back on funding, they just needed to take a look at this prototype first.

As she watched, the prototype's skin rippled and shifted as it gained control over its modifications. Carmen tapped her pen against the desk, watching, watching. One arm turned a dusky orange. Then the other. Until . . .

"Yes!" said Carmen, unable to keep the excitement out of her voice. Aside from the dark stun-band around its neck, the prototype all but blended into the screen behind it.

"Well done, Delta-21," said Carmen, writing a note in the file.

"We're all done for today. Scott will be back shortly to return you to your cell."

When Carmen looked up again, the prototype was standing against the glass, still orange, looking through at the testing room. Carmen leaned closer to the microphone.

"Maybe you didn't hear me, Delta-21. The assessment is over. Put your clothes back on and sit in your wheelchair—a guard will take you back soon."

The prototype crossed its arms over its chest. "My name is Rebecca."

Carmen frowned and looked through the glass at the prototype. "Sure," she said, "you can choose any name you like for your friends to call you, but to me, you will be Delta-21."

"My *parents* called me Rebecca."

Carmen froze, raising an eyebrow. "I hate to break it to you Delta, but you don't *have* any parents."

"Yes, I do. Well, I did. I remember my mother. She had long, blonde hair."

"That's not possible. Maybe you dreamt it."

The prototype stared at her, and, as she watched, its eyes went fully white. It was unnerving.

"Put your clothes on and sit back in the wheelchair, Delta-21," said Carmen, more sharply than she intended, and closed her laptop.

"I told you, my name is Rebecca."

Carmen shook her head and walked out of the examination room, feeling like she couldn't breathe.

CHAPTER 17

Carmen didn't know quite what to make of Delta-21's claims about remembering a life before AWPA. Remembering *parents*.

As far as she was aware, the notion was completely ludicrous. The prototypes were grown in a lab—human DNA mixed with animal DNA—and tweaked until the desired traits were expressed.

She rolled over in her bed, staring at the wall. The moonlight illuminated the edges of her curtain, casting a soft glow throughout the room.

There were a lot of secrets in Project Chrysalis—mysteries around who the financial backers really were, what GenoCorp did with the prototypes, and how the prototypes themselves were created. But parents? The thought raised a whole other level of ethical implications.

Was it even possible to take a fully grown human and alter its DNA? Surely not . . .

Carmen rolled over again, staring up at the ceiling. She had no reason to believe that Delta-21 was telling the truth—after all, it made absolutely no sense if the prototypes had parents. They had clearly been genetically altered, and that could only be done in the foetal stage. Besides, no parent would willingly give up their offspring to AWPA.

Realising that she wasn't going to fall asleep anytime soon, Carmen slipped out of bed and sat at her desk, turning on her laptop. The cursor winked on the blank line of the search engine, waiting for her.

"What are you doing, Carmen?" she muttered, typing in the word *Rebecca*. There were—unsurprisingly—over six billion hits. Celebrities, and novels, and even a couple of films.

Carmen tapped her finger on her desk. She tried *Rebecca prototype*. *Rebecca missing*. *Rebecca gene editing*. Nothing. Then she typed in *gene editing adult*. There were forty-three million results.

Despite Controversy, Human Studies of CRISPR Move Forward

Gene Editing Will Be Used Inside Humans For the First Time

SCIENCE FICTION OR SCIENCE FACT—what does the future of humanity really look like?

Carmen reached for her bottle of wine, and then hesitated. Clicking on the first article, Carmen stood up to put on the kettle.

***

In the end, Carmen decided not to mention Delta-21's claims to Lucinda. All it would receive was a sneer from the lead scientist about how *behavioural* science shouldn't be classed as a science after all. Leave the science to the *real* scientists—Carmen had heard it all before.

Besides, all of her reading had proved fruitless—gene editing in the foetal stage, no problem. Using CRISPR in adults to heal genetic defects—possible, too. But gene editing a person to exhibit enhancements in the league of AWPA's prototypes? That was the work of science fiction.

Friday afternoon, Carmen received a summons to Lucinda's office again. "Twice in one week, lucky me," she muttered, knocking on Lucinda's door.

"Just a minute," called the head scientist, and Carmen could hear voices on the other side of the door.

Sighing, Carmen leant against the wall, hoping the meeting would go quickly so that she could finish up her tests for the day and head home. After working through the previous weekend, she was looking forward to returning to the mainland even more than usual.

The door clicked open and the quality assurance assessor for Zone Three stepped out into the hallway. He gave Carmen a nod, and then hurried long the corridor, looking stressed.

"Great," said Carmen, taking a deep breath before stepping into Lucinda's office.

"Shut the door behind you."

Carmen did as she was told, resisting the urge to roll her eyes.

"Any progress?" asked Lucinda, sitting opposite her.

Carmen shrugged. "Only with the Delta-model, really—it has succeeded in full-body transformation for a single colour. I'll start on more complex backgrounds next week."

"Next week is too late," said Lucinda, even more brusque than usual.

"Okay, well if I reschedule Beta-6 I can continue with Delta-21 this afternoon—" began Carmen.

"I want you to stay this weekend."

Carmen's stomach sank. Of course, that's what Lucinda wanted—more results. "Lucinda, I already delayed my departure by a week . . ."

"I received a phonecall from one of our financial stakeholders today. They are seriously considering withdrawing their investments. I need results, and I need them now." The scientist punctuated her statement with a firm slap of her hand on the desk.

Carmen rubbed a hand over her face. "I'm sorry to hear that, but it's not overly surprising. After the funding was withdrawn from Zone Two, we knew that it could happen again with Zone

One. After all, it's the high-security prototypes that the backers are really interested in."

"I'm not just talking about Zone One," said Lucinda, as though Carmen was the thickest person she'd ever met. "I mean the project as a whole. Zone One, Three, and Four."

"What?" said Carmen, heart beating faster in her chest. "Why?"

Lucinda tapped her fingernail on the desk impatiently, her green eyes piercing into Carmen's own. "Gene editing is expensive. Time consuming. And the benefits are only available to a singular organism. If that money was funnelled into a different avenue—nanotechnology, experimental drugs . . . Cheaper, more time-efficient."

"So what does that mean for us?" Carmen had always known that the low-security prototypes weren't the priority at AWPA, but for the whole project to be shut down . . .

"John and I are heading back to the mainland on Monday to try to talk some sense into them. I know that you are scheduled for two days off this weekend—"

"No, Lucinda."

"You want to keep your job, don't you?"

Carmen narrowed her eyes. Was Lucinda really threatening her? "Of course," she said, carefully.

"And you do realise that right now, if we don't show some results, there won't *be* a job for you in the future?"

Carmen weighed up her response. "Well, I guess I'd better start looking elsewhere."

Lucinda was silent for a moment. "If you don't stay, I'm going to have to find someone else to work with the Zone One prototypes this weekend. They might not be as . . . compassionate as you."

"Is that a threat?"

"Not at all," said Carmen, "just stating the facts."

Carmen thought of the photo frames propped up on her desk. For too long, she'd put this job before her family, before her own wellbeing. "So be it," she said. "Someone else can test the prototypes."

Lucinda looked as though she was going to say something else, but then changed her mind. "Very well," she said at last. "Enjoy your weekend."

Carmen was finally released from the woman's steel gaze.

CHAPTER 18

John wasn't in his office when Carmen knocked, but she sat down at his desk anyway, pulling out her cell phone.

He answered on the second ring. "Hello Carmen, how's it all going?"

"Just wonderful," said Carmen, "I love having my job threatened."

There was a short pause on the other end of the line. "I suppose that Lucinda talked to you," said John. "I'm sorry, Carmen, but there's nothing much we can do about it if the funding is withdrawn. We need to do everything within our power to stop that from happening. Any success with Alpha-3?"

"None," said Carmen. "Headaches and nosebleeds every single time."

"That's a shame," said John, "but I'm sure you'll—"

"I don't want it tested over the weekend," she said. "Not while I'm away."

John was silent, but Carmen could hear something in the background of the call—perhaps the rush of traffic.

"Where are you right now? Can we talk in person?"

"I'm on the mainland. Look, I'll talk to Lucinda, see if we can work something out. She just wants results, you know that."

"Yes, but she won't get any results if she pushes Alpha-3 too far. She can test the other prototypes—the Delta-model is the most promising—but not Alpha-3. It's only going to end in disaster. I know the prototype better than her."

"Indeed," said John. "Anything else?"

Carmen took a deep breath, looking around John's office. There was a photo of John and his two children propped up on a bookshelf, but no pictures of him and Betty. The rumours might be true, then, about their breakup.

Carmen wondered if she should offer him some support— after all, she had gone through the same thing just twelve months ago. But lending an ear to her boss—even if they had known each other for years—was too awkward.

Then she thought of something else. "Let's talk about Rebecca."

"Who's Rebecca?"

"You tell me."

There was a puzzled laugh on the end of the line, and Carmen felt herself relaxing. There wasn't anything strange going on after all, it was just a confused prototype.

"You're going to have to give me a bit more than that to go on, Caz."

"Don't call me that," said Carmen. "Tell me, John, if a prototype told you that they could remember a life *before* AWPA, that they could remember their *parents,* what would you say to that?"

There was silence on the end of the line. "I'd say that's not possible."

"Because the prototypes are made in a lab, aren't they? They are created by AWPA."

"That's right," said John, "I've seen the facilities myself. It sounds like you have a bit of a wishful thinker on your hands."

"I suppose so," said Carmen.

"Think about it," said John, gently. "These prototypes grow up knowing that they have no-one other than AWPA. No parents. No siblings. Nobody who cares about them . . . except for you and me. It makes sense that they make up tales about parents, right?"

"I guess," said Carmen.

"Which one was it, by the way?"

All of a sudden, Carmen didn't want to tell him. "Oh, it doesn't matt—"

"It was the new Delta, wasn't it?"

Carmen took a deep breath. "Yes," she said at last. "It said its name was Rebecca."

"How sweet," said John. "Maybe we should start giving them names rather than model numbers. Make them feel more like individuals. What do you think?"

There was an edge to her boss's voice. "I don't think that's necessary, John," Carmen said, laughing it off.

"Hey, maybe I could name my car? Give it some more personality? Seems to work in the movies."

"I don't—"

"Listen," said John, "I've got to go. I'll catch up with you when I get back. Are you staying this weekend to continue testing?"

"No," said Carmen. "That's why I called, remember—I don't want Lucinda testing Alpha-3 while I'm gone."

"That's right," said John, but he sounded distracted. "Look, I'm not sure that's going to be possible, but I'll try my best."

"Thanks—" began Carmen, but John had already hung up the phone.

***

Carmen packed her bags, and then headed down to Zone One.

One more prototype to assess, and then freedom. According to her schedule, she should be testing Beta-6, but at the last minute, Carmen changed her mind. Scott wouldn't know any different, and if Lucinda checked up on her, she could just say that she changed to Delta-21 in order to get more results.

She waited for Scott to leave the Examination Room before speaking privately to Delta-21. The prototype stared at the crimson screen behind it, eyes narrowed, and Carmen was pleased to see the pigment on its arms rippling and pulsing.

Flicking the cameras off, she moved across the room to the plexi-glass separating the two halves of the testing area.

"Delta-21," she said into the microphone she was holding. "I'd like to speak to you."

The prototype turned towards her, the redness in its eyes fading away to a more natural colour. It raised an eyebrow as it moved closer to the plexi-glass. "What about?"

"About . . . about Rebecca." Carmen felt stupid just saying it. "Your parents. About what you think you remember from . . . before."

The prototype raised an eyebrow. "What are you talking about?"

Carmen sighed. If the prototype wanted her to buy into its story, it really needed to be more open to questioning. "The other day, you told me your name was Rebecca. I'd like to know more about that."

"The other day?"

"Wednesday. When I was testing you. Tell me, Rebecca, what was your last name?"

"I'm not sure what you're—"

Carmen was starting to lose her patience. "I tested you and you told me you remembered a life before AWPA. Or was that just a lie?"

The prototype placed a hand against the glass and Carmen took an involuntary half-step backwards. "Wednesday . . ." said the prototype slowly.

"Never mind about Wednesday," Carmen snapped. "What do you remember before arriving at Zone One?"

Delta-21 leant against the glass, peering through at Carmen. "I remember water," it said at last. "A big river flowing through a city."

"Parents?" prompted Carmen, but the prototype shook its head.

"Just water."

Sighing, Carmen moved back across the room to activate the video cameras and the testing sequence. "Okay, next slide."

CHAPTER 19

Miss Carmen didn't look at Alphie as she wheeled Delta past. Alphie sat back on the floor where she was playing a game with a small millipede that must have climbed up through the pipe at the back of her cell. She put the millipede on the ground with little obstacles made of toilet paper and loose threads from the blanket. Then she watched as it crawled along, seeking freedom.

"Scott," said Carmen. "Has anybody else been working with these prototypes at all?"

"To assess them, you mean?"

"Yes. Or anything really. Has anyone taken these prototypes out of their cells aside from me and you?"

The millipede climbed over top of a toilet paper hurdle and drew closer to the cell door. Alphie picked it up as it reached the bars, and it curled itself up into a ball.

There was a grunt from the corner of the room. "Lucinda came down earlier, took Delta-21 for a checkup in the medical wing."

Silence. "Thanks, Scott."

Alphie heard the click of a door and then a patter of feet on the concrete. Miss Carmen's face appeared outside her cell a moment later, framed by the bars.

"How are you feeling?" she asked, and Alphie shrugged, hiding the millipede behind her back. She wasn't sure that Miss Carmen would be pleased with her playing with bugs.

"Tired."

"What's up with the toilet paper? Don't use it all up or the guards might not give you another roll."

Alphie picked up the piles and scrunched them into a ball, not saying anything.

"Look," said Carmen, "I'm going to be gone for a couple of days."

Alpha-3 nodded, surprised that Miss Carmen was checking in on her again. She must have been *really* worried about her. The thought didn't make Alphie feel any better.

"I'll be back on Monday though, okay?"

Alphie raised an eyebrow. "Okay," she said slowly, not sure what the professor was getting at. She was always back on Mondays.

The professor sighed, rubbing a hand over her face. "Tell me, Alpha-3, do you remember anything before AWPA?"

Alphie frowned. "Do you mean like being created?"

"Anything at all," said Carmen, "before arriving in Zone One." The woman watched her closely, making Alphie feel nervous.

Alphie thought for a moment, lowing her voice. "Is this about Delta? And her dream about the river?"

Miss Carmen nodded. "What about you, Alpha-3? Do you dream about rivers too?"

Alphie shook her head. "I can vaguely remember the helicopter flight, but that's about it. Am I supposed to remember something else?"

"No," said Carmen, taking a step backwards. "That's fine."

"Miss," said Alphie, gesturing for the woman to move closer to the bars.

Miss Carmen hesitated for a moment, and then shuffled slightly closer.

Alphie lowered her voice to barely a whisper. "Delta is a liar, Miss." Alphie didn't know why she said it. The other prototype's comments about Miss Carmen, about Alphie and AWPA, must have been getting to her more than she thought. She felt a bit guilty, but somewhere in the back of her mind she would have loved for Delta-21 to get into trouble. "She even said that you don't really care about the prototypes. But you do, don't you, Miss Carmen?"

"Of course, Alpha-3."

"Then I wouldn't worry about the things she says."

Carmen nodded thoughtfully. "Thank you, Alpha-3." Then she placed her bag on the floor outside Cell One, reached in and withdrew something large and rectangular.

"Here," said Miss Carmen, shoving the book through the small gap beneath the cell doors. Then she stood up and hurried away, the door to Zone One clicking closed behind her.

"What was that all about?" asked Beta-6.

Alphie picked the book up and sat down on the bed, millipede forgotten, and gazed at the cover. She traced a finger over the cartoon pictures. "It's the book of fairy tales that Miss Carmen showed me the other day," said Alphie, unable to contain the wonder in her voice. She opened the cover, exposing felt-tip words scrawled on the inside. *This book is the property of Danielle Templeton*. "It belonged to her daughter."

Beta-6 muttered something in response.

"Nobody's ever given me anything before," said Alphie, stroking the thin pages. "Maybe . . . Never mind." She didn't want to say it aloud, but part of her thought that maybe Miss Carmen thought of her as her other daughter, now. Her non-human daughter.

"Well go on, then," said Beta. "Read us one before the guards come back."

Alphie opened the book to the beginning. "Okay. Story one, Pinocchio."

Alphie smiled as images of growing noses and puppets wanting to be real swirled together in her mind.

CHAPTER 20

Carmen was on her third complimentary glass of red wine when her phone pinged. Glancing around the half-empty plane, she wondered what it would be like to have a normal job. Maybe right now she would be on her way back from a business trip in France or Italy or somewhere else equally as exotic. Maybe the email would be from her boss telling her that she'd done a great job.

But no, she certainly didn't have a normal job, and now she was too invested to truly consider leaving AWPA. She would have to see Project Chrysalis through to the end—whatever that might look like.

She tipped the glass up and poured the last of the wine down her throat before opening the email.

From: <projectchrysalis@awpa.mil>

To: <Rhodes.Carmen@awpa.mil>
Attachments: 0

Subject: Prototype Alpha-3 Update

Carmen,

I have received a response from Lucinda about prototype Alpha-3.

"Why doesn't she just email me herself then," muttered Carmen under her breath. She looked around for a flight attendant to refill her wine glass, but there was no-one to be seen. Lucinda was probably still fuming that Carmen had chosen to take her weekend—a weekend she worked hard for, mind you—rather than staying at AWPA and continuing the tests.

Unfortunately, we both believe that it's in the best interests of the project to continue assessing the prototype throughout the weekend. It's not too late for you to return and carry this out yourself.

Regards,

John

Carmen raised her drink in a mock toast, and then remembered that she had already drained the glass.

She read the email again before swearing under her breath and clicking delete. This was *not* her problem.

Sighing, Carmen reached into her bag, retrieved her private cell phone and checked her messages. It was time to switch off from work and over to 'normal life' . . . whatever that might be. There was a message from her neighbour, Nancy, telling her that the mail was under the doormat. Bless her. The other one was from her son.

Rob's 18th 2nyt. Gonna crash there. Cya 2mro.

Carmen felt her blood pressure rising, but took a few deep breaths before dialling her son's number.

Marcus answered on the third ring. "Hey Mum, whatsupp?"

Carmen shifted in her seat and peered out the window of the plane. "Oh you know, just cruising along at a few thousand feet."

"You know you aren't supposed to use your phone on a plane, right? It can make them fall out of the sky or something."

Carmen laughed. "I'm sure I'll be fine. Hey, so I was looking forward to seeing you tonight. It feels like it's been ages since I last talked to you."

Marcus answered quickly. "Two weeks."

"Right," said Carmen. "Two weeks. And I'm only home for two days so—"

"That's a 'you' problem, not a 'me' problem." His voice had a hard edge, unlike the easy-going manner he usually displayed.

"Look, Marcus—"

"No, Mum. You only want me to spend time with you on your terms. That was fine when I was a kid, but I'm over it."

Carmen took a deep breath. She reminded herself that these weren't her son's words; it was her ex-husband talking, pure and simple.

"I'm going to Rob's, and I'll see you tomorrow, okay?"

"Wait," said Carmen, trying to stop Marcus from hanging up the phone. "I'm sorry. Tell you what, how about we have dinner and then I can drop you at the party afterwards? It can't start until nine or ten surely? Good parties don't start early." She laughed, but Marcus didn't join in.

"We're doing pre-drinks at Susan's."

"Pre-drinks? Marcus, you're only seventeen."

"Bye, Mum—see you tomorrow."

The phone went dead and Carmen bowed her head.

"Another drink, Ma'am?"

So now the flight attendant showed his face. Carmen's head hurt, and she no longer felt like a drink. Carmen gave her empty wine glass to the flight attendant. "No, thanks." Instead, she scrolled through the contacts in her phone, found the one she wanted, and dialled.

"Hello?" A female voice answered, and Carmen stiffened. "Hello," repeated the singsong voice, "anyone there?"

"Umm yes, hi. I'm actually just after Patrick."

"Sweetie," called the woman, "it's for you." *Sweetie?* There was a muffled exchange of words in the background, and then the woman was back on the line. "May I ask who's callin'?" The woman had a distinct Irish lilt.

Carmen bit the inside of her cheek. "Tell him it's his ex-wife."

"Oh."

There was an awkward pause, and then her ex-husband was on the line. "Caz? If you're calling to say you can't have the kids again this weekend, I actually have plans."

"Clearly," said Carmen, thinking of the woman who had answered the phone. And who was *she?* A new addition, or had she been around for a while but nobody had thought to tell her. "Actually, I'm calling to tell you that apparently, our son is going to an eighteenth tonight."

There was a sigh through the line. "Look, Caz, that's for you and him to sort out."

"There's going to be alcohol there." Silence. "Patrick, our son is *seventeen*."

There was a tired laugh on the other end of the line. "Caz, at seventeen you were probably smuggling bottles of red into your room, drinking until you were silly, then climbing out the window to go and join your mates at a dance club."

He wasn't wrong, but that didn't make her feel any better. "I'm losing him, Patrick."

She didn't know why she'd said it. Too many reds, clearly. "Caz . . ."

What did she want Patrick to say to her in return? *No, you're not losing him the way you lost me?* But he didn't say anything. Couldn't, could he? After all, they both knew the truth. She was a terrible mother, and she had been a terrible wife. She'd screwed up the wife part, but maybe she still had some sort of chance on the mother front.

"You haven't lost him, Caz," said Patrick at last. "He's just a teenager, with his whole life ahead of him—plenty of time to hang out with his parents in the future, but only one eighteenth, right? You remember how it was."

Carmen ran a hand through her hair. "Not really," she murmured.

"Look, Marcus has been drafted into the regional football team," said Patrick. "And Danielle's art is on display at the art gallery for a month. You should talk to them about it. It'll give you some place to start."

"Thank you," said Carmen. "Really, thank you."

"Look, I've gotta go. I really do have things on this weekend."

"I know, sorry for calling you."

The line went dead and Carmen lay back in her seat, watching the clouds rush along below her.

***

When Carmen lugged her suitcase up the steps to her apartment, the sun had already begun to set.

"Home, sweet home," she murmured to herself, collapsing onto the couch. Not that her apartment looked at all homely. Carmen would never admit it to anyone else—hardly even to herself—but when she'd first split up with Patrick, she'd thought it was simply a temporary thing. Such a large portion of their lives had been intertwined like a double helix of DNA, and so, when she'd rented this apartment, she'd told herself it was for the short term. She'd only taken out a twelve-month lease because that's what the real estate required, not because she was really going to be apart from Patrick for a whole year.

But here she was, twelve months on, sitting in a living room that still looked like it belonged in a display home. Closing her eyes for a moment, Carmen pictured her past. Just a few short years ago, she would have been sitting in a much-more-chaotic lounge room, the walls plastered with pictures painted by Danielle, and the floor covered with a train track that wound its way around the furniture.

Two small children would have come bouncing up to her the moment she walked in the door, shouting "Mum!" Patrick would have been cooking tea, and the rich smell would have welcomed her home along with her husband's warm embrace.

She opened her eyes, gazing around the white walls. Now, all she got was a cold apartment with nothing to welcome her home except for a pile of junk mail. *Maybe I should get a pet,* thought Carmen. *A lizard. A goldfish.* But no, with her work schedule so unpredictable, she'd never be able to look after it properly. All thoughts of pets would have to wait until she'd left AWPA, or until Project Chrysalis closed for good.

Carmen glanced at her watch. Marcus would be just about to start pre-drinks at his friend's place. She sent a quick prayer to whoever might be listening to keep her son safe. Then she picked up her phone, scrolled down to D and dialled. Her daughter picked up straight away.

"Hey, Mum."

"Danielle, it's good to hear your voice. Sweetie, how's things?"

"Good, good," said her daughter. "How about you?"

Carmen smiled, hardly believing that the twins were basically all grown up. Seventeen. Before she knew it, Danielle would be off to university to carve her own way in life. And Marcus, too—although he couldn't seem to make up his mind about what he was going to do beyond high school. The thought that her children were nearly adults made Carmen feel simultaneously proud and terrified. "Fine, honey. Are you all packed and ready to come stay?"

Her daughter's voice was quiet. "Oh, not yet."

"That's okay," said Carmen, trying not to read too much into it. "Plenty of time. Listen, I was thinking, I really don't feel like cooking tonight." There was a snort on the end of the line, and Carmen had to smile too. Since when did she ever feel like cooking? "So, do you want to go out for dinner? Your pick? Indian? Chinese? I'll come and get you in half an hour? That gives you time to finish packing?"

There was an uncomfortable silence and Carmen's stomach flipped. "Ummm, sorry Mum, but do you think it'd be okay if I stayed over at Rylee's tonight? Her and Brad broke up, and she is in serious need of some girl time."

Carmen could remember Rylee as a little girl with a shock of red hair, coming over on weekends to play with Danielle. The news that she was old enough to not only have a boyfriend, but to be going through a break-up made Carmen feel extremely old.

Unless . . .

"You're not going to that same party as Marcus are you?"

"Yuck Mum, of course not." Her daughter's protest seemed just a little too quick. A little too loud. Or was Carmen being paranoid? Just because Carmen had been a party animal, didn't mean that her own kids were going to turn out the same.

Carmen tried to put on her cheeriest voice as she glanced around her empty apartment. "Okay, hun. You go look after your friend."

"Thanks," said Danielle, "I'll see you tomor—"

"Wait, Danielle," interrupted Carmen. "I wanted to say congratulations."

"What for?"

"For your art being displayed at the art gallery, that's great news."

"Thanks, Mum," said Danielle, sounding pleased. "I didn't even know you knew about that."

Tick one on the good mother list. Only about a billion to go. "Maybe tomorrow we could go check it out?"

A slight pause. "Okay, meet you there at eleven?"

"Sounds great. Ciao."

That went well, thought Carmen sarcastically, looking around the cold, dark apartment. She didn't feel hungry any more but knew that she should eat something. Dragging herself over to the fridge, she pulled the local fish-and-chips takeaway menu off the door.

CHAPTER 21

The weekend progressed in the usual way. First, exercise, listening to the disembodied voice shouting instructions at them in the exercise yard. For once, Alphie didn't want to leave her cell. The four walls contained everything that she wanted in the form of the fairy tale book.

Exercise was mandatory, of course, so before heading outside, Alphie slipped the book between the mattress and the bedframe. Hiding it was probably futile—the eyes on her walls told her that the guards already knew she had it, or would soon enough.

When she returned to her cell, her heart leapt into her throat, but the book was still there. Still there. She stroked a finger lovingly along the spine.

"Cleaning time!" shouted Scott, making her jump.

Alphie stripped her bed and piled the sheets and blanket onto the floor. Her hair had started growing back in after the shave last week, and the thin layer of fuzz was making her itch. She was looking forward to her weekly shower, until she realised that she had nowhere to keep the book of fairy tales dry during cleaning time. Her heart rate increased as she flipped the mattress up on its side against the wall and did her best to jam the book between the leg of the bed and the concrete. She wasn't sure that it would stay totally dry, but there weren't exactly any other options.

"Delta-21," said Scott, from further along the corridor. "It's cleaning time. You need to strip your bed and push the sheets up the front of your cell."

Alphie couldn't make out Delta-21's muffled words, but the prototype didn't sound happy. She hid a small smile, and then visualised the prototype's tearful face as her hair was shaved off last week, and felt bad instead.

"Okay," said Scott. "Centre of your cells. Clothes off."

A woman entered Zone One, pushing a metal cart in front of her. As Alphie removed her clothes and piled them on top of the sheets, the woman used a long pole with a hook on the end to snag the pile and drag them through the opening at the bottom of the cell.

Now there was nothing left in her cell that couldn't get wet—except for the book. She could only hope that the plastic-covered mattress would shield the precious pages from the deluge about to pour from the roof.

"Backs against the bars."

Alphie complied, and after a few seconds, the grip of the stun-band loosened and the collar was pulled through the bars. She rubbed her hands across the raw skin on her neck.

There was a small cry from Delta's cell as the metal nozzles in the ceiling began to shower them all with cold water. Even Alphie—who should have been used to it by now—let out a gasp as the cold liquid cascaded down onto her head. Knowing it wouldn't last for long, she quickly scrubbed the water over her skin, dragging her fingers along her scalp.

Scott was pacing back and forth along the corridor, keeping an eye on them all, and Alphie thought she would risk a question.

"Excuse me, Scott? Any chance I could have some soap?"

The guard looked surprised at her question but returned momentarily with a small block of soap which he threw through the bars. Alphie caught the soap and used it to create a lather on her body, cleaning away the grime. She worked quickly, washing the soap from her arms and legs.

The shower cut off as abruptly as it had begun, and the water ran to the back of the cell in small grooves, eventually flowing down the drain in the back corner. Alphie liked to imagine it flowing through the pipes, taking her skin cells outside AWPA where it might mingle with the water in a drain or stream and end up in the sea. Maybe, somewhere out there, parts of her genetic material were already free.

An old, grey towel was shoved through the hole and Alphie vigorously rubbed her skin as she shivered in the cold air. When her body was as dry as she could get it, she used the towel to remove the water droplets from the plastic outside of the mattress, quickly checking the state of the fairy tale book as she did so. The book seemed to be okay, and she sent a quick thank you to the shimmering light that she'd seen in the examination room. Maybe Delta was right—maybe it wasn't her fairy godmother. But it would do.

Finally, laying the damp towel on the floor of the cell, Alphie stood on it and shuffled forward and back, soaking up as much of the leftover water as she could. Soon, she would receive a pack with a new sheet, blanket, and orange garments to wear for the week. She was looking forward to going to sleep tonight—on cleaning days, she always slept well.

CHAPTER 22

Carmen shielded her eyes from the midday sun, standing on the footpath outside the local art gallery. Glancing at her watch again, she fingered the cellphone in her pocket, but stopped herself from calling. Her daughter would be here soon, surely.

"Hey, Mum. Sorry I'm late."

Carmen turned with a wide smile, reaching out to embrace her daughter. "God, you've gotten big." Danielle was taller than Carmen now, her dyed black hair falling to her waist in perfectly straight locks. She wore dark makeup around her eyes and a fake nose ring. At least, Carmen was pretty sure that it was fake . . . After a moment of hesitation, she decided it was better not to ask.

"Mu-um," said Danielle, giving her mother the perfunctory I'm-seventeen-and-too-cool-for-this hug, "you've been gone for like two weeks."

"Well, you've grown in those two weeks." Giving her daughter a final squeeze, Carmen stood back and surveyed her daughter. Despite the effort that Danielle had clearly put into her hair and makeup, she didn't appear to have put the same level of attention into choosing her clothes. Her daughter was wearing a baggy black sweater and faded jeans that had rips on the knees. She looked tired. Carmen tried not to seek out any hint that her daughter had been out partying all night. "All right, well you'd better show me the masterpiece."

Danielle screwed up her nose and led her mother through the front doors of the gallery. They parted with a gentle *whoof* and admitted the duo inside.

"It's just over here." She gave an embarrassed smile. "It's not very good. I'm not sure why they picked it, really."

Carmen stood at the section marked *Local Artists,* and ran her eyes along the framed pictures on the wall. *Frieda Ross. Annie Rutherford. Danielle Templeton.* "Oh, honey . . ."

"It started out as a school assignment," said Danielle, wrapping her arms around her body as though giving herself a hug. "We had to choose a book that was over a hundred years old as a stimulus. I chose—"

"The Island of Doctor Moreau," murmured Carmen, running her eyes over the evocative reimagining of the classic tale.

"You've read it?" asked Danielle.

"Years ago, back when I was at uni," said Carmen. "It gave me the creeps."

Danielle frowned, and Carmen put an arm around her daughter's shoulder. "It was a powerful book," she clarified, "an important one. I just found it hard to read. But I do love your painting, sweetie." A mad doctor stood beside an operating table where a puma lay, organs exposed for all to see. Danielle had painted it in the style of an old 1950s movie poster, and Carmen hadn't been lying when she said she loved it—it really was very good. "It's the best one here."

Danielle blushed under her thick makeup. "You have to say that—you're my mum."

"No," said Carmen, "I'm serious. Can I buy it? I'll hang it in my office."

Danielle laughed, but she looked pleased.

"Where *do* you get your talent from?" Carmen squeezed her daughter's shoulder.

"Not from you or Dad, I know that much," said Danielle, laughing. "Dad can't even draw stick figures. Do you want to have a look around the rest of the gallery?"

Carmen nodded, allowing her daughter to lead her through to the main display room. For a small town, the art gallery maintained a high standard of exhibits. She supposed it had to—what else was there to do in a town that didn't even have a movie theatre?

"Were Grandma and Grandad into art at all?" asked Danielle, as they perused a display of twisted metal.

Carmen shrugged, then shook her head. "I don't know. I don't think so."

Danielle read the description on the metal exhibit. "These are all made of car parts," she said in wonder, "just kind of Frankensteined together. It must have taken ages."

"They would have been so proud of you, you know," said Carmen with a sad smile. "I wish they could have met you."

Danielle was silent. Carmen wondered if it was possible to miss someone that she'd never even met.

"You know, Mr Garney said if I keep working on my portfolio, I might be able to study Fine Arts at university next year." Danielle glanced sideways at her mother, as though unsure how Carmen would take this news.

"I think that sounds wonderful." Carmen decided not to mention that the closest Fine Arts school was only an hour train ride away.

Danielle visibly relaxed and allowed herself a proper smile. "I thought you might have wanted me to . . . you know . . . follow in your footsteps or something. Study science."

"I studied behavioural science because it called to me," said Carmen. "And no way, you study whatever interests you."

Her daughter tugged at the bottom of her faded shirt, looking at the ground.

"What is it?"

"It's just . . ." She shrugged. "Dad says that a BFA stands for . . ." Danielle gave an uncomfortable little smile.

"Spit it out."

"Well, a Bachelor of Fuck All."

Carmen bit the inside of her lip until she thought she'd be able to speak without insulting her ex-husband. "Don't worry about your father," she said at last. "He's just bitter because he was forced by his parents to study an accounting degree—which he hated, mind you. I'll talk to him."

"Thanks, Mum. And you're happy with what you studied? You enjoy working at the hospital for refugees?"

Before Carmen could answer, the jarring notes of some alternative song blared from Danielle's pocket. She withdrew the phone and looked at the caller ID before lifting it to her ear.

"Finally awake, are you? How's the hangover?" She paused for a moment, her face draining of colour. "Sorry, what?"

"Is that your brother?" asked Carmen, but her daughter just turned away.

"Yes, I'm his sister. . . Okay, I'll be there soon." She hung up the phone, visibly shaken.

"Danielle, what's going on?"

"It's Marcus," said Danielle, walking swiftly towards the exit of the art gallery.

"And? Where are you going? Danielle, answer me."

"Hurry up!" said Danielle. "We have to go to the hospital."

CHAPTER 23

Miss Carmen was going to be away for the entire weekend.

Which meant no assessments—no headaches—for two whole days. Alphie smiled up at the grey ceiling, connecting the little pockmarks on the roof with invisible lines to create pictures in her mind.

There used to be another professor like Miss Carmen who would run tests too, even on weekends, but he disappeared a long time ago. So, with Miss Carmen gone back to her home for a few days, she was going to be left in peace.

The door to Zone One clicked open and Alphie's stomach rumbled. Tearing her eyes away from the ceiling—where she had just worked out how to connect a bunch of small dots to create a tree with a fluffy top—Alphie stood with her back against the far wall of the cell as required at mealtimes. But the woman who appeared in the corridor outside Alphie's cell wasn't dressed in the black uniform of the guards. Instead, she wore a long, white coat like the doctors and scientists. Her hair was pulled up in a high bun flecked with silver streaks.

"Hands where I can see them," said the woman, and Alphie raised her hands in the air, feeling confused.

Perhaps the woman was there to conduct a medical check-up, thought Alphie. Investigating the headaches, perhaps. After all, Miss Carmen had told Alphie that she was going to have some time off to recuperate. Surely she wouldn't be tested this weekend—not by this woman, at least.

Alphie tried to make out the name on the ID card hanging from a blue lanyard around the woman's neck. If only she had Beta's eyesight . . .

"You," said the woman, and Alphie jumped. But she wasn't talking to Alphie—a guard with dark, short-cropped hair appeared outside her cell. It was the same nervous woman who had helped Scott in the exercise yard for the past week.

"Yes, Lucinda?" The woman was clearly still uneasy being around the prototypes, but desperate to please.

"I'd like you to enter the prototype's cell."

Alphie saw the guard's face blanch under the dim lights. "But Mr Haven said—"

"John isn't here right now."

The guard's gaze flicked from Lucinda to Alphie, and then back again.

"Well, Nikki, you've been given a very clear instruction from your superior. You don't want to lose your job in your first week, do you?"

Nikki stood still, and then slowly shook her head.

"Please enter the prototype's enclosure."

Alphie pressed herself further back against the wall so as not to intimidate the guard and give her any reason to use the stun-band regulator that she was already retrieving from her belt. Unlocking the cell door, the guard was visibly shaking as she pushed it open with a high-pitched squeak.

"Move over to the bed," said Lucinda, and Nikki did as she was told.

It was only when Lucinda instructed Nikki to lift the mattress that Alphie realised what was going on. "No," she whispered, as the guard picked up the book of fairy tales and then backed out of the cell. Alphie's eyes blurred with unshed tears.

"This doesn't look like appropriate reading material, does it, Nikki?"

The guard shook her head, carefully pulling the cell door shut and checking the lock. Lucinda took the book from Nikki and held it out in front of her, opening it to a page in the middle. Tut-tutting, she made eye contact with Alpha-3 for the first time since she had entered Zone One.

"Do you want this back?" she asked Alphie.

Alphie froze, biting her lip so hard that she drew blood, trying to work out the appropriate response. Slowly, she shook her head.

"Very well," said Lucinda, gripping the top of one page and tearing it downwards. The sound made Alphie feel like her soul was being torn in two—not just the pages of a book.

"Wait," she said, clearing her throat. "Wait."

Lucinda stopped ripping the page and looked at Alphie expectantly. "Yes?"

"I do. Want it, that is. I do want it back."

"Good," said Lucinda. "I'll be back this afternoon to assess you. If you can show me some results, then you get the book back. If you can't . . ." The scientist made a show of ripping the page another centimetre and Alphie trembled. "Understand?"

Alphie nodded, sniffing. "Yes, Miss. I understand perfectly."

The woman moved down the corridor, her high-heels making a clicking sound as she walked. "And you. Delta. You're up first, straight after lunch. Prepare to be exceptional."

"Oh, I will be," said Delta-21, her voice filled with ice.

***

"It's just a stupid book," said Delta for the third time.

"It's more than that," said Alphie, still shaking from the brief encounter with Lucinda. "It was a gift from Miss Carmen."

"So? Miss Carmen doesn't really care about you. She just wants results."

Alphie lay on her bed, highly aware of the emptiness between her mattress and bedframe.

"It's good that Miss Carmen wants results," said Gamma. "That way, maybe Alphie will finally be picked by GenoCorp. She's been here longer than all of us."

There was murmuring around the rest of the cells, and then Beta spoke up. "I'm more worried about what this woman is

143

going to do to Alphie, than what she's going to do to a book," he said.

Alphie's heart beat faster. "What do you mean?"

"She seems . . . different than Miss Carmen. Like maybe she wouldn't stop if you got another headache. She'd just keep pushing. Like she wants to rip more than just a page."

"Quiet," said Zeta.

The prototypes fell silent, and then the nervous guard with short-cropped hair re-entered Zone One. Nikki. This time she was wheeling a metal trolley along with her. Nikki moved all the way to the end of the corridor and peered into Alphie's cell. Alphie slid off her bed and backed against the far wall, raising her hands again to show that she wasn't planning on doing anything brash.

The guard bent down, placed a tray of food on the ground, and slid it through the gap in the lower bars.

"Come and get it," said the woman. She seemed a little more relaxed now. Perhaps her confidence had been bolstered by her experience of entering a prototype's cell and *not* dying an untimely death. Nikki returned to the trolley, picked up another plastic tray, and then walked over to Beta's cell. Alphie heard the scrape as the tray was pushed into the cell next door.

Alphie picked up her own lunch and peered down at the assortment of colours. Something grey, something white, and something an off shade of orange. Alphie was never too sure what it was they were being fed, but she didn't complain. There was no point. Sitting on the edge of her bed, Alphie took a bite of the white thing. Potato, perhaps. She watched as the guard returned to the trolley parked in front of Alphie's cell twice more in order to feed Gamma and Delta. How long would it be, she wondered, before Lucinda showed up to take her to the examination rooms? She wished Miss Carmen was here. Did she even know what Lucinda was planning to do to Alphie?

The guard didn't return from Delta's cell for a long time. Alpha listened, and she thought she could hear a strange, strangled noise accompanied by the light clang of something against metal.

"Delta!" Epsilon's shocked voice had Alphie on her feet instantly, almost knocking her food flying. "Delta, no!"

Alphie moved as far across to the edge of her cell as she could, trying to peer along the corridor to see what all the noise was about. She could just make out Nikki's legs pushing against the ground, trying unsuccessfully to move backwards, away from Delta's cell. The strangled, choking sound was louder now, interspersed with a cheer from one of the other prototypes—Gamma or Zeta, perhaps.

"What on Earth—"

The door to Zone One flew open with a bang. "Drop her." Michael entered the corridor, aiming his gun into Delta's cell. The gurgling sound continued.

Scott raced in behind Michael. "Don't shoot," warned Scott. "You might hit Nikki. Activate the stun-band instead."

Michael bent down and picked up something off the ground that Nikki had dropped—the stun-band regulator—and a moment later Delta's high-pitched cry echoed around the low-security zone. Delta released the hands she had around the guard's throat and Nikki slumped to the ground.

Alphie couldn't hear what the men were saying to Nikki as they checked her over and helped her to her feet, because Delta's cries drowned their words out. Scott helped the woman out of the door while Michael flicked the switch on the small regulator. The cries turned to silence, which seemed even louder, somehow.

"That was very stupid," said Michael, his voice low and menacing.

Ragged breathing from Delta's cell echoed around Zone One. "I was just doing what you wanted, wasn't I?" asked Delta. "Learning to control my abilities? I even managed to fool a guard—I think you could call this a success."

Alphie pressed against the bars, holding her breath as her blood pumped through her veins ferociously. Nobody had ever attacked a guard before, not ever. Michael was right—it was just plain stupid. And of course it would be a Delta who would finally take a step too far.

"You don't like the stun-band much, do you?" asked Michael. "Well, maybe this'll help you learn your lesson." He turned the switch on the regulator, and Delta-21 started to shout again, then cry, then just whimper as Michael laughed coldly. "A couple of hours of that, and maybe you'll think twice about attacking another guard."

CHAPTER 24

Carmen's phone buzzed again, and she swiped to decline the call.

"Was that Dad?" asked Danielle, from a chair on the other side of the hospital bed. She gazed anxiously at Carmen across her brother's sleeping form.

"No," said Carmen. "If it was, I would have answered. He should be here by now." Carmen leaned forward and touched her son's hand, noting the bruises tracing contours along his arm, disappearing beneath the hospital gown.

"I can't believe he'd be so stupid," said Danielle.

"Your brother or your father?"

Danielle raised an eyebrow but didn't say anything, and Carmen decided to keep her mouth shut.

The recklessness of her youth seemed like a distant memory. Those in glass houses and all . . .

There was a commotion at the door of the hospital ward, and then Patrick was striding into the room, straight past Carmen, to stand at the foot of their son's hospital bed.

"Finally," said Carmen, rising to her feet. "Where were you?"

Patrick's gaze flickered to Carmen and then back to Marcus, concern creasing his brow. "I told you, Caz—we went away for the weekend. We rushed back as fast as we could. Fiona dropped me off at the emergency entrance and she's still parking the car."

Fiona. So that was the name of his new woman. Carmen's phone buzzed again, and she slid the bar across to decline. Why the hell was work calling her private phone? That was just a step too far.

"Are you going to take that?" asked Patrick.

"It's been going off for ages," said Danielle. "Somebody really wants to talk to Mum. Work." She scrunched up her nose.

"Work can wait. I have slightly more important things to be worrying about," said Carmen, moving across to Marcus's side.

"For once," said Patrick, and Carmen narrowed her eyes. "So what exactly happened?" Patrick gazed at the clipboard hanging off the foot of the hospital bed as though he understood what was written there.

"Got in a car with his mate," said Danielle.

"His mate who had been *drinking,*" said Carmen, glaring at Patrick.

"Look, Caz, this isn't the time to be playing the blame game—"

"Isn't it?" asked Carmen, voice rising. "Because my son is lying in a hospital bed right now—"

"*Our* son."

Carmen's phone buzzed again, disturbing the tension.

"I think you should take that," said Patrick, voice quiet, filled with suppressed emotion.

Carmen glanced at Marcus's sleeping form as she put the phone back in her pocket. "No."

"There's nothing you can do here right now," insisted Patrick, clearing his throat. "I'll let you know if he—"

Patrick's phone rung loudly in the hospital ward, and Danielle rolled her eyes. "Really, guys? And you say that it's *our* generation who's obsessed with technology."

Patrick frowned at the phone and then accepted the call. "Hello?" He glanced over at Carmen. "Yes, I'm with her."

Carmen went cold.

"Okay." Patrick held the phone out to Carmen. "I believe that it's for you."

Carmen hesitated, then decided that the only way to get work to leave her alone was to answer the call. Patrick was right—there was nothing she could do for Marcus right now, and besides, she really needed a coffee. She nodded, accepting the phone and stepping outside the ward.

"Hello?"

"Caz, where have you been?"

"John, what the hell are you doing calling my ex-husband's number? My *private* number? That's a step too far."

"Sorry, but—"

"And where do you *think* I've been?" She started walking quickly along the corridor. "At home. It's Saturday. I do have a life outside work, you know." She thought about her night in the hot tub with fish and chips and a glass of wine. She thought of her son, lying unconscious on a hospital bed. Some life.

"Well, did you read my emails?"

"No."

There was a hissing sound on the end of the line, like air going out of a punctured tyre.

"I can hang up and go and read them now, if you like." Carmen glanced up at the signs on the wall and turned right, following the arrow towards the hospital café.

"Carmen, get yourself to the Point Lansell helipad straight away, we have a situation."

"What sort of situation?" She imagined Alpha-3, lying dead on the bottom of a cold cell and she felt sick. Lucinda had pushed the prototype too far, hadn't she?

"We've had a break-through."

This was not what Carmen was expecting to hear. As she passed one of the waiting rooms, she saw a coin-operated coffee machine squatting in the corner. She diverted her journey—any coffee would do. "Okay," she said slowly, hoping she wasn't going to regret her curiosity. "I'm listening."

"Delta-21 injured a guard."

Carmen pinned the phone between her shoulder and ear as she took one of the polystyrene cups and placed it beneath the coffee machine. Then she fished in her coat pocket for a two-dollar coin.

"Gee, what a break-through. Look, it's the weekend, and I have a bit of a situation right now, so—"

"I don't appreciate your sarcasm, Carmen. Aren't you interested in *how* the prototype managed to get close enough to injure a guard in the first place?"

Carmen *was* interested—there were clear protocols to protect the staff—but still, whatever John said wasn't going to make her leave her family and get back onto that helicopter. Recent events with Marcus told her that she was needed at home.

Still, she figured that there was no harm in finding out what had happened. "Fine," she said, sighing heavily and pressing the button on the coffee machine. A fragrant brown liquid began pouring into her cup. "What happened?"

"Nikki—the new guard—was feeding the prototypes lunch. Orders were clear, keep the prototypes far away while you push the food through."

"Uh-huh," said Carmen, "guessing someone got a bit too close to a Delta model." The coffee machine beeped, signalling that her drink was ready.

"So she looks inside the cell," continued John as though Carmen hadn't said anything, "and Delta-21 is in bed still, with a blanket over top of it."

Carmen took a sip of the coffee and grimaced at the bitter taste. "Let me guess," she said, heading back along the corridor to the hospital ward. "Actually, the prototype was hiding behind the bed, ready to launch forward and grab Nikki the moment she pushed the tray under the cell door."

"Not quite," said John. "The prototype was actually right in front of her, lying on the ground."

"I don't under—"

"The prototype changed, Carmen. And it did such a good job of blending in with the floor of the cell that Nikki didn't see it there."

"Is Nikki okay?"

"Yes, yes of course." Carmen could hear the indignation in his voice. "I'm not a monster, Carmen. But are you listening to me? A Delta-model finally did something really impressive. A low-security prototype achieved something that none of us ever thought it could. It blended into a complex, real-world environment."

Carmen rounded the corner and saw a woman standing with Patrick outside Marcus's room. Great. "Thanks for your faith in my zone, John."

"You know what I mean." John's voice softened. "Look, Carmen, when we shut Zone Two, you knew that Zone One might not be far behind. The low-security prototypes just never produced the same results as the high-security ones. But this is your chance—our chance—to show everyone that Zone One *should* be noticed. It might be enough to get the stakeholders to extend their funding—for Zone One, and for the entire project."

Carmen hung back from the cosy reunion that was happening outside her son's hospital room. When the woman with fiery red hair threw her arms around Danielle, Carmen turned away. "Look, that's great, John, I look forward to working with the prototype on Monday."

"Carmen," said John, clearly exasperated. "I'm doing my part, preparing for a final meeting with the stakeholders—a meeting that will hopefully save not only your job, but my job too."

"Aha."

"You're only a two-hour helicopter flight to AWPA. If you leave now, you can conduct tests all afternoon and tomorrow, and I can share the results with the financial stakeholders on Monday. It might just be enough to renew their interest."

Carmen took a seat in the waiting room, making sure that she was in clear sight of Patrick so that he could let her know if Marcus woke up. "Look, John, I meant to say this earlier, but I was never too sure when was an appropriate time. I'm sorry to hear about you and Betty."

"What?" The surprise on the other end of the line was so clear, that Carmen wondered if she had got her wires crossed.

"Uh, I heard that the two of you split up. Unless . . ."

"Yes, we did, but it was a long time coming. Carmen, what's that got to do with our current predicament?"

"John, you have kids, same as me. And maybe, just like me, you let work dominate your life and affect your relationships too. It's basically a year to the day since I split up with Patrick . . . My kids need to come before work. And maybe yours do too."

That's what she should have said a few years ago. Was it too late, saying it now? The recent image of her son's bruised and battered face told her that maybe it was.

"Dammit Carmen, just listen to me. There won't *be* any work for you if we can't show some results."

Carmen sipped again on the bitter coffee. "They aren't going to shut the project down in one day, John."

"Look, Carmen—"

"No." It felt good to say it. "I'm spending some time with my kids this weekend and that's that."

"Carmen—"

"Leave the prototype in its cell—or let Lucinda test it, if she's so keen. I'll be there tomorrow night."

CHAPTER 25

The screams became cries, then the cries became whimpers, as the stun-band delivered a constant stream of electricity into Delta-21. For what felt like hours, Alphie listened as Delta alternated between throwing herself against the bars and groaning quietly.

"Maybe you could tell her a story," suggested Beta, and Alphie started to recount the tale of Thumbelina.

"No," said Delta, panting heavily. "I don't need your stupid fake tales. They won't make me feel better." Then she groaned and was silent for a long time.

"I think she's passed out," said Epsilon.

"Probably a good thing," said Beta. "I can't imagine what it must feel like, the pain going on for so long. The small zaps are bad enough."

The other prototypes murmured their agreement.

"Or maybe she's dead," said Gamma, and she sounded like she was about to cry.

Alphie wanted to point out the truth—that Delta-21 had brought this punishment on herself. After all, none of the other prototypes had ever been subject to such cruelty, but they had never tried to injure a guard, either. She bit her tongue, knowing that her observations wouldn't go down well. With this sort of behaviour, maybe Delta-21 would never join GenoCorp. Maybe it would be Alpha-3 who was next on the list.

"I think we could still tell stories though," said Beta-6. "I mean, there hasn't been a guard here for hours—they must be too preoccupied sorting out the mess that Delta-21 created."

"Do you think she killed the guard?" asked Alphie.

"I hope so," said Epsilon.

"I don't—"

"Shhh," said Zeta. The sound of the door opening interrupted any further conversation, Alphie heard the clonk of feet as somebody entered Zone One. She glanced through the bars and saw that it was Scott. He paused outside Delta's cell and peered in, looking confused.

"What's wrong with you?"

No answer.

"Delta-21, if you're faking this in an attempt to lure another guard near your cell, you've got another thing coming."

Silence.

"Epsilon-10, do you know what's wrong with Delta-21?"

"Michael left the stun-band activated," explained Epsilon, sounding surprised that Scott would talk to him. "She's been screaming for hours, and now . . ."

Alphie watched Scott carefully, wondering what his response would be. Face pale, he grabbed the regulator hanging from his belt and jabbed a button. Nothing changed audibly, but Alphie thought she felt the tension dissipate as he switched off Delta-21's stun-band.

Raising his transceiver, Scott glanced into Delta's cell. His eyes were wide, and Alphie wondered what he could see. There was a crackle of static, and then, "I need a doctor to Zone One. Now."

CHAPTER 26

"Caz?"

Carmen looked up at Patrick from her position in the waiting room, fearing the worst.

"Marcus is awake."

"Oh, thank God." Carmen followed Patrick into Marcus's room to see Danielle giving her brother a long hug. When she stood up, her dark makeup was smeared across her cheeks.

"How are ye feelin'?" asked the woman, Fiona. Carmen found her Irish accent grating.

"Sore," said Marcus with a grimace. "What happened?"

"You were in a car accident," said Patrick. "Gave us all a scare."

"I was?" Confusion clouded Marcus's face as he sorted through his memories. "Dave! Is Dave okay?"

"Dave's fine," said Patrick. "Drove into a fence, though. The fence isn't so fine."

Marcus grinned and then winced. "Ouch. Don't make me smile."

Carmen felt her blood pressure rising. "I don't think this is the time for jokes."

All four turned towards Carmen as though just noticing her for the first time. Fiona's arm was around Patrick's waist—the perfect little family.

"You could have *died,* Marcus."

His face darkened. "I'm sorry."

"You're *sorry*? What were you thinking?" All of the fear that had been growing throughout the day bubbled to the surface and poured out as anger instead. "Oh that's right—you weren't."

"That's not fair," began Marcus.

"Isn't it? Have we neglected our parenting duties so much that you didn't know not to get into a car with a drunk driver?"

"Well, if we're going to start talking about neglecting parenting duties—"

"I think—" said Fiona.

"You can shut it."

The woman's cheeks approached the same colour as her hair. She whispered something in Patrick's ear and then left the room.

"Look, Mum, stop freaking out and listen to me, okay?" said Marcus, trying to sit up. His face contorted with pain, and Danielle stepped forward, slipping a pillow behind her brother's back. "I didn't deliberately get in the car with a drunk driver."

"So what," said Carmen, "you tripped and fell into the car?"

Marcus shifted his attention to his father. "Do I have to listen to her?"

Patrick muttered something non-committal and Carmen gritted her teeth.

"Too right, you have to listen to me. I'm your mother."

"When you feel like it."

Marcus glared at Carmen while Patrick tried to calm the situation down.

"How about we all just—"

"Look," said Marcus, "Dave was drinking last night at Rob's party, sure. We all were. We crashed the night at Rob's place, then when we woke up this morning, we all just felt a bit hungover. I didn't even think about the fact that Dave might still be over the limit. He probably didn't either. It was a mistake—a stupid mistake, but I'm okay."

There was a bump the size of a large marble on Marcus' temple, and Carmen felt her emotions well up and threaten to overflow down her cheeks.

"Now, can you apologise to Fiona, please—she's actually really nice. I think you'd like her."

Carmen stalked out of the hospital room, unsure what her plan was other than to get out of there. She felt so many things at once—frustration, fear, anger—that she didn't quite know where to start.

Her stupid, stupid son. But he was okay. He was going to be okay.

She walked along the corridor and noticed Fiona's red ponytail as the woman inserted money in the coin-operated coffee machine in the corner of the waiting room. Sighing, Carmen walked up to her. "I wouldn't, if I were you."

Fiona looked up at her, eyebrow raised.

Carmen gestured towards the machine. "I had one earlier. I'd rather drink battery acid. Come on,"—she gestured down the hallway—"I'll shout you a real coffee." It wasn't explicitly saying sorry, but it was the best that Carmen could come up with right now.

"That's all right," said the woman, pressing the button on the coffee machine. "I don't mind drinkin' battery acid." An awkward tension hovered in the air between them.

"So, how long have you and Patrick been together?" asked Carmen, in what she hoped was a nonchalant tone.

The woman gave her a sideways glance as the cup filled with coffee. "Just a few months. I wasn't the reason for yer breakup with Patrick, if that's what ye were thinkin'."

Carmen mumbled something along the lines of "of course not," feeling the colour rise in her cheeks.

"Ye've got some wonderful children," Fiona continued. "They're a credit to you both."

Was that a jibe about Carmen's regular absences, or was she being serious? Carmen couldn't tell, and as Fiona started walking back to the room, Carmen decided not to ask.

CHAPTER 27

"Can you hear me?" asked the doctor, standing in the corridor, well away from the door of Cell Four.

Alphie peered through the bars and almost smiled at how nervous both the doctor and the guard were. Almost. The fact that Delta-21 was lying unconscious—or worse—just a few feet away, drained any possibility of humour from the situation. She might not *like* Delta, but that didn't mean that she wanted her dead.

"Can you open your eyes?"

Silence. The doctor and Scott exchanged an unreadable glance.

"Do you think you should go in there?" asked Scott. "Check if it's breathing?"

"Are you offering?"

Scott shrugged, glancing through the bars. "I suppose not. Not if it can become virtually invisible at will—that sounds like a recipe for disaster."

"We could try and shock it again?" suggested the doctor. "If it's unconscious, that might wake it up."

There was a groan from Delta's cell, and then a raspy, "Don't you dare."

Alphie couldn't help smiling, and both Scott and the doctor visibly relaxed. Their precious prototype hadn't been killed at least. The doctor opened a bag on the floor, pulling out a clipboard.

"My name is Ian," he said matter-of-factly, "and I'd appreciate your co-operation as I assess your health."

"My co-operation?" replied the prototype, her voice quiet. She coughed, and Alphie thought she heard a splatter of something on the floor of the cell. "There's blood in my mouth and piss on my pants, but sure, I'll co-operate."

"Excellent," said Ian, as though he hadn't noticed her tone. His held a pen poised above his clipboard. "First up, what is your name?"

"Delta-21," replied the prototype, in gravelly tones.

"And where are you right now?"

"I'm in hell."

Neither the doctor nor the guard laughed at Delta's comment. Perhaps they were smart enough to realise that it wasn't meant to be humorous. Retrieving something from his bag, the doctor took a half-step nearer to the cell, and then shone the beam of a torch in through the bars. "Pupil response normal," he murmured.

"I'm surprised you can tell from that far away," said Delta. "It might be easier if you actually came inside my cell, you know."

Ian's skin paled. "Looks alright," he said to Scott. "I don't think there's been any brain damage from the prolonged voltage."

Scott looked relieved. "When I saw it lying on the ground like that . . . Still, we'd better take it in for a proper assessment."

The doctor nodded and reached for his radio. "I need a gurney to Zone One."

Then he reached into his bag and pulled something out that resembled a small gun.

"What's that?" murmured Delta-21. "You going to shoot me now?"

"It's just a sedative," said Scott.

"Maybe Michael could have used that instead of half-killing me."

"You attacked a guard," Ian pointed out. "You don't get a say in how you are disabled."

Scott aimed the small device into Cell 4 and pulled the trigger. Alphie braced for a loud bang, but there was only a click, and then silence.

"Wait for it," said Scott. "Wait."

The two men stared through the bars. "Okay, let's go."

As Scott unlocked the cell, the door at the end of the corridor opened, and a bed was wheeled into the area. Alphie watched with curiosity as the three men unceremoniously shoved Delta-21 onto the gurney. Her limbs flopped over the sides of the bed, and the doctor roughly grabbed her and tied her down.

"Goodbye," whispered Alphie, as the prototype was wheeled out of Zone One. "Good luck."

***

In all the commotion with Delta-21, Alphie had forgotten about her imminent meeting with Lucinda. It was only when her hand drifted unconsciously to the space between her mattress and the bedframe that she remembered the woman's threats.

Part of her hoped that Lucinda would be too preoccupied with the other prototype to worry about Alphie, but she was also determined to prove herself and get the fairy tale book back. *If* the woman was telling the truth.

"Beta." Alphie's voice was low as it inched through the metal grate. She heard a shuffle on the other side of the wall as Beta-6 moved closer to her.

"Yeah?"

"Do you think Delta will be okay?"

"I don't know." His voice sounded faint, like he was speaking from far away, and not just from the cell beside her.

"She sounded so sick—"

"I said, I don't know, Alphie." There was an edge to his voice, and Alphie decided not to push it.

"Someone's coming," said Zeta, and Alphie's spirits rose, hoping that it was Delta-21 returning to her cell.

The door to Zone One clicked open, and then Scott was outside Alphie's cell, waiting to scan her wrist.

"Is Delta alright?" she asked in a small voice, slipping her hand through the bars.

"Prototypes are not to ask questions." It wasn't Scott who answered her, but a woman standing just out of sight. Lucinda.

Her stomach sunk. Alphie thought she might have seen the hint of an apology in Scott's eyes, but perhaps that was just wishful thinking. Scott unlocked the cell door as Lucinda brought the wheelchair over, and then they both stood back as Alphie took her seat. With a shiver, she remembered what Beta-6 had said about Lucinda tearing her mind apart like the page of the fairy tale book.

The bonds clamped firmly around her wrists, and then Lucinda pushed her through the doors and along the corridor to Examination Room Two. The woman didn't speak one word to Alphie as they entered the room. Pushing the wheelchair up to the table, she opened a laptop and positioned it in front of Alphie. Then she activated the video cameras and looked at Alphie expectantly.

"Miss Carmen usually attaches a screen to the wheelchair," said Alphie.

"I'm not Miss Carmen," said Lucinda, her voice sharp. "You can work with the data on my laptop instead."

As Alphie watched, a series of symbols began tracking across the screen—white on a dark background.

"It doesn't say anything," said Alphie, confused, as the disjointed digits disappeared and new ones began to take their place. "Is it supposed to say something?"

"Just watch," said Lucinda. "See if you can work it out."

Alphie concentrated on the text on the screen, trying to commit it to memory, trying to decipher some sort of pattern. The symbols moved quickly, and without any sort of context she felt panic rising in her. In the past, there had always been some sort of order to the data, or at least a form of rules. Words were made of letters. Maths equations formed solutions. But these symbols—lines and dots—appeared in a seemingly random jumble.

"Concentrate, Alpha-3," said Lucinda, "or you know what the consequences will be." The woman gestured to the storybook sitting innocently on the edge of the desk.

Alphie returned her attention to the screen, but now the symbols had been replaced with something else—a sort of loopy scribble that looked like nothing she had ever seen before. "I don't even know what this is," she said, feeling tension in the back of her head like she did when the headaches were coming. "And I'm starting to get a headache already."

"That's not going to work on me," said Lucinda. "We will keep going until there are results."

"It's just squiggles," said Alphie, her voice rising. "How am I supposed to work it out if I can't even read it in the first place?"

"Perhaps this will help," said Lucinda, pausing the program and pulling a small black container out of her bag. Placing it on the table, she opened it up to reveal a syringe filled with clear liquid.

"What is that?"

In the corner of the room, a faint light started to flicker and coalesce into an immaterial form. Alphie gazed at the orb, a sense of warmth spreading through her body. It was her guardian angel, she was sure of it—here to rescue her from the clutches of the evil scientist.

Lucinda seemed unaware of the being in the room, and Alphie almost laughed aloud. The people who worked at AWPA, they all thought they knew everything about what was going on in the world. They all sought to control and test, and control some more. But here was something outside even Lucinda's jurisdiction.

"Cinderella will go to the ball," murmured Alphie, as the bright light approached. The pressure increased in the back of her head, but it wasn't painful—at least, not yet.

Lucinda depressed the plunger on the syringe and a fine spray of liquid emerged from the tip. Then she rose, skirting around the table until she was beside Alphie. "This will help you to concentrate," she said, pushing the sleeve of Alphie's shirt up and wiping something cold across the skin on her upper arm. "It's imperative that we get some results."

Alphie closed her eyes, wishing with all her might to be out of this place. No more tests. No more Lucinda. Any moment now, the bright light would surely change shape and encircle Lucinda, stopping her in her tracks.

Alphie screamed as the sharp tip of the needle pierced her skin and cold fire spread throughout her arm.

CHAPTER 28

"Go home, Caz," said Patrick, and Carmen's eyelids fluttered open.

"I'm awake," she said, stifling a yawn. Her back ached from sleeping in an uncomfortable position in the chair beside Marcus's bed. The glowing digits on her watch told her it was only 4pm—it felt a lot later than that. Marcus was sitting up in bed, flicking through channels on the television suspended from the ceiling, while Danielle sat on the far side of the room, sketching in her notebook as the afternoon light filtered through the window.

"There's no point in us all being here," said Patrick, reasonably. "They want to keep Marcus in overnight and we can't all sleep here."

"Fine," said Carmen, stretching. "You and Fiona take Danielle home and I'll stay here with Marcus."

Her son's gaze flicked from the TV, over to Carmen, and then back to the screen again. "No thanks."

Carmen bristled and glared at Patrick.

"Son—"

"I'm fine here by myself," said Marcus.

At the same time, Danielle announced, "I'm not going anywhere."

The siblings shared a glance.

"Fine," said Marcus. "Danielle can stay, but you lot can all leave. I'm fine, really—it makes me uncomfortable having you all staring at me in my PJs." He flicked the television to a music station and rock music blared from the speakers.

Carmen frowned and he turned it down a couple of notches.

"Besides, some mates are coming over soon. Dave and some others. It's a small room—there's not enough space for all of you."

"Dave's done enough—" began Carmen.

"He's my *friend*."

Patrick stood up, and Fiona followed suit.

"What?" said Carmen, not moving from her seat. "You're leaving?"

"You heard the boy," said Patrick. "Danielle's here—she'll call us if there's any issues. Marcus is fine—just a few bruises and a bump on the head. Let him spend some time with his friends."

"Spending time with his friends," said Carmen, gripping the edges of her seat, "is exactly what got him into this mess."

The phone in Carmen's pocket vibrated, and she pulled it out to see a text message from John.

Issues with Alpha-3. Possible retirement. Call me.

She took a deep breath, reading the text again. Retirement. Bloody Lucinda. "I need to take a call, but this is not over."

The waiting room had people in it now, so Carmen stalked straight past them to the door marked 'courtyard.' It was cold outside, but it suited her mood. Carmen pulled her jacket closer around her and sat on a wooden bench on the far side of the courtyard, dialling John's number.

"Hi, Carmen."

"So let me get this straight," she began, keeping her voice low. "I'm gone for a day, and not only does a prototype attack a guard, but Lucinda has taken this opportunity to push her agenda of retiring Alpha-3? Have I missed anything?"

"It's not like that," said John.

"You're the boss, John—not Lucinda. You're the manager of Project Chrysalis—or did you forget that for a few years?"

"Calm down—"

"I will not calm down," said Carmen, rising to her feet and pacing back and forth along the courtyard. "I'm in a hospital *on the weekend* after my son had a car crash and here you are, threatening to retire Alpha-3?"

"I'm not threatening anything," said John. "And I'm sorry to hear about your son. Is he okay?"

She took a deep breath. "He's going to be fine. But John, what is this? Alpha-3 will show results, I know it will."

"Actually," said John, "it won't. Not at this rate—it's currently in a coma."

Carmen stopped pacing, seeing black spots in her vision. "If this is some tale to get me running back to AWPA to test Delta-21—"

"It's not a lie," John reassured her. "Alpha-3 is currently lying unconscious in the medical wing."

"Jesus, John." Carmen glanced around the courtyard, keeping her voice low. "What did you do to my prototype?

***

There was a helicopter waiting at the Point Lansell helipad when Carmen's taxi pulled up. Paying the driver, Carmen hurried across the tarmac to the chopper, crouched like a large mosquito on the helipad.

All the way from the hospital, to her apartment, and now to Point Lansell, Carmen had been second-guessing her decision to return to AWPA. Marcus had assured her that he was fine—that he'd prefer her to go, actually—and that he'd see her next weekend. Danielle had suggested that they go out for Indian next Saturday night. *All* of them.

"That's a wonderful idea," said Fiona, giving Carmen a far-too-familiar squeeze and telling her not to worry about Marcus. Some people could rock the split family thing, but Carmen wasn't so sure that she would survive a single dinner with her ex-husband and his gorgeous new girlfriend. She tried her best to shift her view—the kids seemed to really like Fiona, and anything that would help to ease the pain of their parents' separation was surely a good thing. Even if it created more pain for her.

"ID?" said the woman waiting by the door of the helicopter. Carmen fished the lanyard out of her bag and flashed it at the pilot. Satisfied, she gestured to Carmen to hop on board.

Carmen climbed into the helicopter and stowed her single bag of luggage under the seat. Doing up her seatbelt, the pilot started the engine and soon the deafening sound of the rotor blades above them rendered all conversation impossible. This suited Carmen just fine, and she sat back in the seat and tried to relax.

The machine tilted slightly, Carmen squeezed her eyes shut, and a moment later they were up in the air. Carmen travelled by helicopter regularly, but that didn't mean that the queasy feeling in her stomach had gone away. She usually only travelled from the AWPA facility to the mainland—after that, she would board a plane to travel the forty-five minutes or so to her home town. Clearly John thought this was no time to be waiting for planes.

Alpha-3 is in a coma. She hadn't managed to get much more information out of John except that Lucinda had been working with the prototype when it had a seizure. Bloody Lucinda. The woman was fixated on getting results at any cost. Had she accidentally pushed the prototype too far, or had she simply decided to retire the prototype and start afresh with Alpha-4?

As they flew across a patchwork quilt of farmland, Carmen's thoughts drifted to Delta-21. *There's been a breakthrough.* That's what John had said. Finally, something spectacular would be coming from a Delta-model, even if it had taken an injured guard to get there. The image of Delta-21 being able to control its abilities so well that it could fool a guard excited Carmen to no end, almost drowning her concern about Alpha-3. A breakthrough in the low-security zone? It was almost unthinkable.

Carmen had often heard the assessors from the high-security zones whispering about some secretive advancements they were making, and Carmen had just nodded along with them, pretending that she was making significant progress too. They must have known better because they never asked Carmen any follow up questions. She was just in the low-security wing. None of her prototypes would ever really amount to much.

Except that this time, one had. And it wasn't even the Alpha-model as she had imagined.

Carmen started to form a plan for her arrival at AWPA— first, she would visit Alpha-3 and make sure they weren't retiring it anytime soon. Then, she would spend the evening working with Delta-21. She would skip straight ahead to the more complex tests involving forests and deserts and cityscapes.

It was going to be a long night. Carmen sighed and wished that helicopters came with free booze.

CHAPTER 29

The moment the helicopter touched down at AWPA, Carmen was summoned to the office of one Doctor Ian Reed. Trying not to let the annoyance show on her face, Carmen dropped her suitcase off at reception to be taken up to her room. Perhaps the doctor would be giving her some answers about why Alpha-3 was in a coma.

It was Lucinda who answered the door to the doctor's office when Carmen knocked, and she resisted the urge to groan aloud.

"Nice to see you back and ready to work," said Lucinda. Carmen could hear the accusation in her voice.

"Hello, Lucinda," Carmen said with a nod. She would be quite happy if she didn't have to talk to Lucinda ever again. "Haven't you done enough damage?"

"Excuse me?"

Carmen forced herself not to wither beneath the woman's glare. "Shouldn't you be preparing for your meeting with the stakeholders?"

Lucinda's mouth twitched, but there was nothing else to give away her emotions. "I'm leaving this evening. I have some things to finish off here first. Come in."

Some things to finish off. Like Alpha-3.

Entering the office, a man in a white coat turned to greet Carmen. "Ian," he said, by way of introduction, clasping her hand in a weak shake. "Take a seat." He gestured towards two chairs on the far side of his desk.

"I'd like to see Alpha-3," Carmen replied, crossing her arms across her chest and making no move towards the seat. "And then I'm ready to begin assessing Delta-21. What am I doing here?"

"We seem to have a problem with the prototype," said the doctor, gazing at her from behind thick-rimmed glasses. "Please, sit down."

"Yeah, being in a coma is quite a big problem," said Carmen, already regretting her decision to return to AWPA."

"Not a problem with Alpha-3," said Ian. "It's Delta-21."

Carmen finally did as she was told, and Lucinda sat next to her. Carmen looked around the small room: charts displaying human body parts that looked far too real leered off the walls towards her; a jar on Ian's bookshelf was filled with some sort of nasty looking liquid and brown lumps.

"As I said, my name is Ian," said the doctor, sitting down opposite the two women. The thick lenses of his glasses made his eyes seem unnaturally large. "I usually work with the high-security prototypes, but we have a bit of a unique problem with Delta-21, so I came on board." Ian's fingers tapped lightly on the wooden desk as though he was nervous.

"Okay," Carmen said slowly. "What sort of problem? I thought we'd had a breakthrough."

"Oh we did," said the doctor. "Quite marvellous really—I've never seen anything like it. You should see the footage—"

"Ian," said Lucinda, pointing at her watch.

"Yes, yes, all right, the problem. Well, you see . . ." The tapping on the table became more furious, and Carmen frowned, trying to work out what was going on. "When Delta-21 attacked the guard—"

"Nikki," interrupted Carmen, shooting a glare at Lucinda. "Why does nobody seem to remember the poor girl's name?"

"Yes, when it attacked *Nikki*, another guard decided to retaliate. He went against protocol—left the stun-band on high voltage for far longer than we would ever recommend." He gave a nervous laugh.

"How long?" asked Carmen, wondering where this was going.

"Hours," said Lucinda.

"Right," said Carmen, leaning back in her chair. "So Michael decided to electrocute my prototype—to torture it for hours on end."

"I never said it was Michael," said Lucinda.

"You didn't say it wasn't. Did he get fired at least?"

Lucinda's lips tightened. "He received a warning."

"Great," said Carmen, rolling her eyes. "So what's the damage? Are you saying I can't start assessing straight away?"

Ian clasped his hands in front of him as though he wasn't sure what to do with them. At least he'd stopped tapping for now. "The prototype is currently in the hospital wing."

"What?" said Carmen. "I'm gone for a day and not one, but *two* prototypes end up in the hospital wing. Jesus."

The doctor just stared at her.

"Well, is it awake? Or is Delta-21 in a coma as well."

"Oh no," said Ian. "It's wide awake. The damage wasn't physical—well, at least the physical aspects aren't long term."

"What, then?" asked Carmen, as Lucinda and Ian shared a glance. "Psychological? The prototype has gone completely insane? I can still work with it . . . probably. I've worked with crazy prototypes before."

"It reports that it can't change anymore, Carmen," said Lucinda at last. "The electrocution may have . . . *damaged* its abilities."

Carmen felt her blood pressure rising. "If it can no longer change its appearance then what am I doing here?"

Ian turned his computer monitor around and showed it to Carmen. "This is a scan of Delta-21's brain," he explained. "I've done some preliminary tests, and there doesn't seem to be any reason why it *can't* change. You know the prototype better than any of us—"

"Yeah, right—"

"You know the Delta line," interrupted Lucinda. "They are all much of a muchness."

"—so we hope that you will be able to have better success than the other quality assurance assessor who tried."

"Besides," said Lucinda, "it was asking for you."

Lucinda held a light brown folder out to Carmen, and she took it, slipping a photograph out from between the covers. The image was a little grainy, but Carmen could easily make out the bars of Cell Four. A guard—presumably Nikki—was in mid-stride, walking towards Delta-21's cell.

"Take a close look, Carmen," said Lucinda. "Delta-21 is lying right there on the ground, blending so perfectly with the concrete that you can't make it out, even if you know it's there."

Carmen peered into the photo at the space in front of the bars. All she could see was concrete—there was no hint that a prototype was lying right there, waiting to attack the guard. "Amazing . . ." she breathed. "You can't even see its stun-band."

"It must have lain with its hands across its neck. It's clever, I'll give it that."

"But you're saying that it can't do this anymore?" Carmen slipped the photo back into the file.

"You've always been very persuasive, Professor Rhodes. I'm sure you will work something out."

"And if I can't?" asked Carmen, eyes narrowing. "I suppose that's good enough reason to finally terminate my contract?"

Lucinda sighed. "Don't be so overdramatic."

"This is ridiculous," said Carmen, rising to her feet. "If Delta-21 is injured, retire it already. You seem pretty ready to do that to Alpha-3."

"Alpha-3 is in a coma, Delta-21 is not."

"Yes," said Carmen, "Alpha-3 *is* in a coma. Shall we talk about why?"

The older woman stared at Carmen, eyes narrowed. "You weren't here—we needed results."

"And all you got was a prototype in a coma. What did you do? Keep pushing it after it started getting a headache?"

"Ah, if I may interject," said Ian, hands twitching, "There is a possibility that it had a reaction to 453."

"453?" asked Carmen.

The doctor nodded, as though assuming that Carmen knew what the hell he was talking about.

"Ian, what is 453?"

"Oh, well sometimes the prototypes seem to struggle with their enhancements," said Ian, "and not just Alpha-3. We've seen it in the older Delta models, and some of the high-security prototypes as well—it's as though their bodies are rejecting the DNA." He looked positively excited by this notion, and Carmen raised an eyebrow. "Sometimes it manifests in stomach cramps, aches and pains, migraines"—he nodded towards Carmen as though proving a point—"or even less obvious ways that aren't perceived until we do a blood test or a CT scan. It's fascinating, really, how it all works."

"Indeed," said Carmen. "But what is 453?"

Ian leant forward, resting his elbows on the desk, his eyes appearing to bulge out of his skull. "I have been working with a team to create a serum that assists in bonding the introduced DNA with the existing DNA—early trials on rodents have proved most revealing."

"Rodents?" Carmen could imagine rats engineered to glow in the dark or smell food from ten kilometres away. She shivered, turning towards Lucinda. "Aha, and you used it on Alpha-3? Even though you knew it might not work."

"I had no choice," said Lucinda.

"There's always a choice."

Lucinda shifted her chair slightly, leaning back with her arms crossed over her torso. "How long have you been working with Alpha-3?" she asked.

Carmen shrugged. "Years. So what?"

"Right," said Lucinda, "and do you think in all these years, perhaps you've gotten just a little too close to the prototypes— particularly Alpha-3—to remain objective?"

"Lucinda, are you really questioning my dedication to this company?"

"Professor, it's not your dedication that I'm questioning. It's your ability to remain impartial that has always concerned me."

Carmen bit back all of the retorts that rose to the back of her throat.

"When John hired you, I had my suspicions that you were too soft-hearted, too governed by your emotions. That's why I started you off on probation in the retirement ward, rather than in quality assurance where you are now."

"I know," said Carmen, "but I passed your little probation test. John moved me to Zone One years ago."

"I know he did," said Lucinda. "But I did some digging. Turns out you knew John before you began work at Project Chrysalis."

Carmen went cold. "I did. We went to university together. Have you been re-reading my résumé as you consider promoting me to a high security zone? Zone Three or Four, perhaps? I'm well overdue for a promotion."

"Not exactly," said Lucinda. "You're a hard woman to find information on, Professor. But I have contacts in many places. You weren't just friends with John, were you?"

Carmen stood up, banging her leg painfully against the table as she did so. "That's none of your business—"

"Sit down, Professor."

Carmen couldn't help it—she did as she was told.

Lucinda reached down into her bag. "Perhaps you can explain this?" She placed the book of fairy tales on the desk in front of Carmen.

Carmen felt the heat rising in her cheeks. "It's not—this was just a way of motivating the prototype," she stuttered.

"Bullshit," said Lucinda. "There was a reason I started you off in retirement and not assessment. There was less possibility for you to get attached. If I had my way, you would have stayed in retirement and never received a promotion."

Carmen sat silently, dumbfounded at this turn of events.

"So what is this, a termination meeting?"

"Not at all," said Lucinda, "if you can get some results."

"From the comatose prototype or the crazy one?"

Ian laughed and then tried to cover it up with a cough.

"From Delta-21," said Lucinda, drily. "By the time I get off that plane on the mainland, I expect some good news to share with the stakeholders."

"And if it really can't use its abilities anymore, if they've somehow been shattered by prolonged exposure to pain, what do you expect me to do?"

"Pack your bags," said Lucinda, rising from her seat.

Carmen bristled. "I'll be talking to John about this."

"I'm sure you will," said Lucinda. "But just remember that it'll be all of us packing our bags, not just you. The quality assurance assessors in the high-security zones are working just as hard, don't worry. In the meantime, Ian will set you up with a supply of 453."

"So, let me get this straight," said Carmen, standing up. "This serum. 453. You want me to give it to Delta-21? Even though you know it might have the same effect as it had on Alpha-3?"

"We don't know that," said Lucinda. "We don't really know why Alpha-3 is in a coma."

"Yeah, right," said Carmen, turning towards the door.

"But yes, if you can't get any results from Delta-21, then I would like you to administer the serum."

"Two comatose prototypes in one day? That sounds like a good way to win the support from the stakeholders." She placed a hand on the doorknob.

"It's taking up our resources, you know, to keep the Alpha-model in the hospital wing. I could turn it off now, if you like—or do you want to be the one to flick the switch?"

Carmen looked back across the room, from Ian to Lucinda. "Fine," she said. "I'll do whatever it takes to get Delta-21 to show some results." Walking back over to the table, she reached for the fairy tale book. "But first, I'd like to pay a visit to Alpha-3.

***

Carmen was still seething as she walked back and forth along the corridor outside the medical wing. How dare Lucinda suggest that Carmen had only received her position because of a prior relationship with the project manager? How dare she suggest that Carmen wasn't good at her job? And what was she doing, digging into Carmen's past . . .

She sighed, rubbing a tired hand against her temple. As she walked, her shoes made a gentle clip-clop sound on the linoleum floor. She imagined that they were slowly wearing down the white lino until one day she would fall right through. In her left hand, she gripped the fairy tale book, but every time she went to open the door to the ward, she seemed unable to do so. She visualised Alpha-3's small body, looking even more vulnerable lying on a hospital bed.

Steeling herself, Carmen turned and reached for the door, but it swung open before she had a chance to enter.

"Carmen, it's good to see you." John stepped out of the ward and into the corridor, his face visibly brightening when he saw her.

"John," said Carmen with a nod. "What's the verdict with Alpha-3?"

He shrugged, leading her along the corridor a short way as though he didn't want the comatose patient—or the medical staff—to hear what he had to say. "It's not looking good, Carmen."

Carmen felt her hand gripping the fairy tale book shake slightly. "For Alpha-3 or for Project Chrysalis?"

"Both," he said with a wry smile. "Are you examining the Delta-model this evening?"

"Yes," said Carmen, "and I have orders to *do whatever it takes*." The sarcasm was clear in her voice, but John didn't seem to notice it.

"Good, good," he said absently, rubbing a hand across his lined face. He was dressed in a suit and tie, more suited for a business meeting than checking on a patient.

Carmen turned back towards the door, taking a deep breath. Her feet felt like they were fused with the linoleum.

John watched her with interest. "If you stay here, waiting outside the hospital ward, worried about a prototype, you are just proving all of Lucinda's concerns valid."

"And what concerns are they, John?" asked Carmen, her voice rising so that John hushed her. "No. I'm good at my job—and part of the reason that I'm good is because at some level I *do* care about the prototypes. I don't see that as a bad thing, even if Lucinda does."

"Come on," said John, taking Carmen by the elbow, "I'll come with you."

Carmen sidestepped out of John's reach. He raised an eyebrow and then walked back into the medical ward, holding the door open for her. Carmen took a breath of antiseptic-tainted air and then walked inside, thinking that there were too many hospitals and doctors in her life right now.

Alpha-3 was the only patient, covered in tubes and lying quietly on a bed.

"She looks so small," whispered Carmen.

"It," corrected John.

"No," said Carmen, shaking her head. "She." Carmen tore her gaze away from the sick prototype and turned towards John. "I can't believe Lucinda would do this to my prototype."

"She didn't do it intentionally, Carmen—she just wants results, same as all of us."

John looked down at Carmen's hand, but made no move to touch her again. "You know, I was devastated when you chose Patrick over me."

Carmen didn't respond.

"We had some good times, Carmen."

She nodded absentmindedly. "Lucinda thinks you only hired me to work here because you knew me," said Carmen.

John didn't respond, and Carmen decided not to push it—she didn't really want to know the truth after all.

"Before you broke up with me," said John, "all those years ago—I knew in my gut that it was over."

Carmen touched the prototype's arm lightly. Its skin felt human. "We always had different approaches, John. But why are you telling me this?"

"Look, the stakeholders might not have pulled the plug yet, but I can feel it in my gut, the same as I could back then. It's over, Carmen. Project Chrysalis is going to be *retired*."

Goosebumps rippled across Carmen's arms. She moved closer to the prototype, looking down into its face. "You don't know that."

"Perhaps not," said John, "but I'm making an educated guess. They have other, more immediate projects to pour their money into that achieve the same—if not better—results."

Carmen thought about this for a moment. AWPA had been such a big part of her life for so long, that the idea of it finally closing down was unfathomable. "And if the project is over, what happens to Alpha-3? To all the prototypes."

"You know what happens—you worked in retirement for long enough. You can do the deed with this one, if you like."

Carmen felt sick. "We need to wait twenty-four hours. See if it wakes up. That's policy."

"Yes, it is. But euthanising the prototype while it is unconscious and has no awareness of what is happening is kinder than doing it when it is fully awake. And if we do it now, we can get one more set of data from it to try to please the stakeholders."

Carmen's skin crawled. "You always were motivated by results," she said quietly. "That's where we are different." She reached out and ran a finger lightly across the prototype's forehead. She looked so peaceful.

"Go away, John. Go and meet with your beloved stakeholders and see what you can do. I will begin work with Delta-21 shortly and forward you any results."

John turned towards the door.

"Oh, and John? Even if this somehow all pulls through, if the financial backers decide to maintain their investments and Project Chrysalis continues? I'd like you to accept my formal resignation."

John opened his mouth as though to say something, thought about it, and then silently walked out the door.

CHAPTER 30

Delta-21 was standing in the centre of Examination Room Three, already naked, when Carmen arrived.

"Hello, Miss Carmen," it said, arms crossed over its chest.

Carmen could see red marks on its neck around the edges of the stun-band from the steady stream of electricity. Bloody Michael. Carmen couldn't believe that he'd only received a warning.

"Sorry to drag you back here on your day off." The prototype's tone of voice suggested that it was certainly *not* at all apologetic.

"I heard that you were asking for me." Carmen sat down at the desk on the other side of the plexi-glass, placing a small, rectangular box on the edge of the table.

"What's that?" asked Delta-21.

"Insurance," replied Carmen. Opening up her laptop, she navigated to the sharepoint and accessed the first file in the examination folder. A little pang of disappointment stabbed through her—all the way here on the helicopter, Carmen had imagined being able to start with the more complex tests, of seeing the prototype all but disappear in front of her eyes. Bloody Michael.

Clicking the play button on *Deta.Test1,* the screen behind the prototype filled with a warm brown hue. The prototype's face sagged. "Didn't they tell you, Miss Carmen? There's no point. I can't change any more."

"They told me," said Carmen, leaning forward to speak into the microphone, "but I've seen the photo, Delta-21. I know what you can do."

"Could do," the prototype corrected her. "I've tried—I can't do it anymore."

"We'll see," said Miss Carmen, as the colour behind the prototype changed to a soft teal.

Delta-21 glanced at the colour, then made a show of trying to concentrate. It screwed up its eyes, balled its fists and all but shook with effort. Then it relaxed, looking mournfully through the plexi-glass. "See, Miss Carmen. It's impossible. Something must have happened to my abilities when I was left in my cell for so long in pain. It's like something just switched off." The prototype gazed imploringly through the plexi-glass, its eyes an indeterminate shade of grey. "You may as well just retire me now, Miss Carmen—don't waste any more time on me."

Carmen couldn't help but laugh. "What exactly do you think retirement is, Delta-21?"

The prototype stared at her.

"Do you think it's a white picket fence and a house with a pool? Oh Delta-21, I thought you were smarter than that." Carmen turned the microphone up loud so that it would pick up her voice from across the room. Rising, she retrieved the rectangular box from the desk and walked towards the plexi-glass.

The prototype moved backwards as though it was afraid of her. The screen shifted to a royal shade of blue and Delta-21 crossed its arms across its chest, glaring at Miss Carmen from the back of the room. "So what's retirement, really?" asked Delta. The light from the screen lit up its cheeks in a strange blue hue. "And if I don't have any abilities any more, what will you do to me?" Was there a waver of fear in its voice?

Carmen slid open the box and lifted the syringe into clear view. The light glinted off the sharp sliver of metal.

"What's that?" asked Delta-21.

"I'll leave that up to the imagination," said Carmen. "But let's just say that it's the reason Alpha-3 is lying comatose in a hospital ward right now. If you don't start showing some results, I have orders to use it on you."

The prototype's dark skin shivered for a moment and Carmen watched closely, seeing if there was even the slightest hint of a change. The image on the screen shifted again to a new image, but rather than being a single colour, this one was more complex. It took a moment for both Carmen and Delta-21 to realise what it was showing.

"What the hell?" said Delta-21, staring with wide eyes at the image of four people gazing out of the screen.

Carmen dashed towards the laptop and slammed the lid closed. The disturbing image winked away to blackness.

Her heart hammered in her chest as Delta-21 glared at her, and the prototype's eyes turned fully black.

"I'm going to kill you, you know?" said Delta-21. "I'm going to bloody kill you."

***

Carmen stood outside the examination room, her back against the wall, sucking deep breaths into her lungs. Pulling her phone out of her pocket, she sent a quick email to John with the subject 'WTF' and then walked back along the corridor.

She didn't pay attention to where her feet were taking her, echoes of 'I'm going to bloody kill you' swirling around in her mind. The look on Delta-21's face . . . where the hell had that image come from?

She would keep going with the tests. She had to. But right now she needed to go for a walk. Or have a drink.

Carmen pulled her phone back out of her pocket and dialled. "Ward 2. This is Mary."

"Mary, it's Carmen—"

"Alpha-3 has not yet regained consciousness, Professor Rhodes. As I told you half an hour ago, you will be the first one to know if it wakes up."

"When," said Carmen, "not if."

There was a short laugh on the other end of the line. "Look, Carmen—the seizure went for seventy-two minutes and it failed to respond to benzodiazepines or anaesthesia. That's long enough for the excitatory neurotransmitters to damage the neurons."

Carmen understood enough to know that was bad. "So you don't think the prototype will recover?"

"It might, given long enough. But I have my orders from Lucinda. Six hours and we euthanise and do an autopsy."

"Six?" repeated Carmen, fear gripping her belly. "No, John said twenty-four."

"Those are my orders," said Mary. "And those hours are almost up. The surgeons are beginning their preparations. John did say to give you the option to administer the injection, if you like."

Carmen leaned heavily against the wall. "No." The hand holding the phone trembled slightly. "No, I don't think I can do that."

Mary's voice softened slightly. "Look, I know you've been working with the prototype for years. If you want to be here at the end, that's fine—even if you don't want to retire it yourself."

Carmen thought for a moment, teetering on the brink. She imagined Alpha-3 lying on the hospital bed, taking her last breath. "No," she said at last, "I have other things to do." *Like finish assessing Delta-21.*

"That's fine," said Mary. "If Project Chrysalis is to continue, we will start preparations for Alpha-4 once Alpha-3 is gone. If not, well, they are all going to be retired anyway. There's no blood on your hands, Carmen. You don't need to feel guilty."

"I don't," began Carmen, but she knew it was a lie. Hanging up the phone, Carmen glanced up to see that her feet had taken her to the entrance of the low-security zone.

When Carmen entered Zone One, Zeta-7 glared at her. She gave it a nod, wondering if it could hear Carmen's heartbeat right now, increasing in tempo as she walked along the corridor. It would be such a shame if all the prototypes were retired.

She stopped outside Epsilon-10's cell, looking in. The prototype was covered in bandages, some showing spots of crimson blood. It was a fascinating specimen—when the Epsilon-models were performing to their true potential, an entire limb could be removed without them feeling anything.

Then came the cell where Delta-21 would usually be found. Carmen hurried past Cells Three and Four, and arrived at the cell she was here for. Beta-6 looked up at her with an accusing look on its face.

"You killed her." It wasn't a question. "You killed Alphie." Its—his—eyes were glistening with tears, his face red and blotchy. "She trusted you."

"I didn't kill her," Carmen began to protest, but then she stopped. Alpha-3 might not be dead yet, but she soon would be. Carmen felt a wave of nausea, and she placed a hand on the wall behind her to steady herself. "I'm sorry," she said at last.

"And what about Delta? Is she dead too?"

Carmen shook her head. "No, Delta is okay. For now."

There was a strangled cry from somewhere further along the corridor, and Carmen felt her stomach twist. "I know you don't believe this, but I *do* care about you Beta-6. And I care about Alpha-3 too. I care about all of you."

"Yeah, right," said Beta. "Unlock this door then, and we'll never trouble you again."

"You know I can't do that."

The prototype sat down on the floor and put his head in his hands.

"Alpha-3 isn't dead," said Carmen at last. "But she *is* in a coma." On a whim, she added, "Is there anything you want me to tell her before the end?"

"I just don't want her to die alone," said Beta, his voice muffled behind his hands.

"She won't," said Carmen, wondering if she was telling another lie. "I'll be there for her."

"Tell her . . ." said Beta, looking up at Carmen, "tell her that we all lived happily ever after. She'd like that."

Carmen nodded, feeling like she couldn't breathe. "I will." Wiping her eyes, she scurried back along the corridor and out of Zone One.

CHAPTER 31

From: <projectchrysalis@awpa.mil>
To: <Rhodes.Carmen@awpa.mil>
Attachments: 0

Subject: WTF

Carmen—please use a more professional email subject in the future.

Thank you for alerting me to the rogue image in the Delta examination sequence. A full inquiry has been launched into where the photo originated from and how it ended up in the test. Some disgruntled employee clearly decided to play around with some image editing software. And to what end? Rest assured, we'll work it out.

In the meantime, please continue examining Delta-21 and forwarding me all results.

Regards,

John

Carmen finished reading the email and then put her phone away, glancing around the small operating theatre.

"This is ridiculous," said Ian, glaring at Carmen. "You shouldn't be here."

Carmen smoothed out the white surgical gown Mary had given her and adjusted the mask on her face. "John said I could be here."

"John said you could administer the injection, not come in and read it a bloody fairy story."

"Ian," said Carmen, raising her eyebrows, "you'd already be hacking into its brain by now if you'd just let me start reading."

Carmen could imagine Ian's mouth twisting up beneath the mask, but all she could see were his narrowed eyes. "Fine. But hurry up."

The surgeons stood around the edges of the room, waiting to play their part in the end of prototype Alpha-3.

Carmen had thought about which story she would read to Alphie in her final minutes. She had never thought to ask which story was her favourite—all she knew was that the prototype didn't like Hansel and Gretel. And then it had seemed so obvious. Sleeping Beauty.

She began to read, looking up now and again at Alphie's sleeping form, hoping that she would wake up. But of course, there was no prince to wake her from this sleep.

". . . he came across a maiden of great beauty. She lay as if asleep, and her long, fair hair wrapped around her body like a mantle. Her eyes were closed, but her chest moved with the slightest breath, leaving the prince no doubt that she was alive."

Carmen sniffed, glancing at Alphie's body, covered in tubes. In the tray beside the bed lay the injection, already prepped and ready to go. No, Carmen couldn't do it—but she *could* be here in the prototype's final moments.

"And so she lived happily ever after," finished Carmen, closing the book lightly as silence descended upon the room. "They all did," she added in a whisper.

"Okay," said Ian, all business. "Let's get this show on the road."

CHAPTER 32

Somebody was talking just near her, but Alphie couldn't make out the words. The sound was muffled and seemed to be coming from a great distance as Alphie felt herself drifting back to sleep.

"Cut through the—"

"—and then we'll inspect—"

"—we'll euthanise in one minute and then—"

A searing pain ricocheted through her head and Alphie sat up with a groan. Something sharp tugged at the skin on her arms and she swiped blearily at the tubes that were sprouting all over her body.

"Woah, not so fast."

Alphie focused slowly on the scene in front of her. Three people in white lab coats were gathered around the bed she was lying on.

"Alphie," said a familiar voice from the end of the bed and Alphie focused on the person sitting near her feet. She couldn't recognise the woman with her mask and lab coat on, but she would be able to know that voice anywhere.

"Miss Carmen, what's going on?" she said slowly, noting a table of sharp implements beside her. A machine somewhere to her left began to beep quickly and a moment later Miss Carmen was by her side, telling her to relax—that it was all going to be okay.

"Never mind," said the doctor closest to her, "check it over and then return it to its cell."

Alphie groaned again, putting her head in her hands.

The woman leaned in. "My name is Mary. Can you talk? How many fingers am I holding up?"

"Three," said Alphie, rubbing her eyes as Mary shone a torch into them.

"Pupil dilation normal," said Mary.

Alphie lay back on the bed and tried to remember what had happened to her. The past just seemed to be a long, dark tunnel.

"What's happening, Miss Carmen?"

The professor ran a hand across her face. "You had a seizure, Alpha-3. You went into a coma."

"And are you all trying to fix me?"

The professor didn't answer. Instead, she turned towards the nurse. "I need to keep assessing Delta-21. After you finish your check-up, is the prototype cleared to return to its cell?"

"Yes, go. We'll arrange for a guard to return the prototype to Zone One," said the nurse.

Alphie frowned. "That woman—Lucinda—she gave me something. An injection . . . Are you going to give me that again?"

"No," said Carmen. The quality assurance assessor reached forward, tucking the book of fairy tales beneath Alphie's arm. "I'll see you soon," she said. "I promise."

CHAPTER 33

Carmen couldn't help grinning as she walked back to the assessment rooms. Alpha-3 was alive—for another day, at least. And then tomorrow, they would all find out the fate of Project Chrysalis.

She had expected Delta-21 to still be raging when she returned to continue the assessment, but the prototype was sitting placidly on the floor in the centre of the observation room. It didn't look up when Carmen sat at the desk and projected a white background onto the screen.

"Was that photo real?" asked Delta-21, still staring at the ground.

"No, Delta-21," said Carmen. "Just some clever photo-manipulation."

"It looked like me." Delta-21 looked up, and its eyes had returned to dark grey. "I didn't recognise the other people, but that was definitely me."

Carmen didn't respond. "It's time to continue our assessments," she said lightly.

"But that doesn't make any sense, does it, Miss Carmen? That *can't* be me. I was created by AWPA in a facility on the mainland and then transferred here, right?"

"Right," said Carmen.

"No time to meet up with other people and take a photo," continued Delta. "Particularly a photo that I don't recall ever being taken."

"It was just a cruel joke by someone on the mainland who creates the testing sequences," said Carmen. "I guess they thought it'd be funny to add it in and throw you off. Don't worry, they'll be found out and their employment will be terminated."

"The water in the background," continued Delta, "now *that* looked familiar. A big river rushing past the city."

Carmen tried to ignore the uncomfortable feeling in her stomach. "Okay Delta, show me what you've got."

Delta-21 remained on the ground, yawning. "I just feel so tired, Miss Carmen, I don't think I can do it today."

Carmen pressed a button on the regulator and the prototype's head snapped back. It jumped up, raising its hand to the stun-band.

"Feeling more awake now, are we?"

Delta-21's eyes narrowed as it glowered at Carmen through the plexi-glass. The prototype shook its head, crossing its arms. "Not today," it said.

Carmen pressed the button again and Delta-21 fell to the floor, limbs jerking erratically. "Don't you understand, Delta-21? If you don't perform, then the whole project will be shut down."

"Good," gasped Delta-21, from its position on the floor.

Carmen administered another shock, but still, the pigment in its skin didn't change. The prototype put a hand to its stomach as though it was going to throw up. It retched a couple of times and then wiped a hand across its mouth.

"What do you think will happen to you if Project Chrysalis is shut down?" asked Carmen.

The prototype rose to its feet and looked at her with pure hatred. "You tell so many lies, Miss Carmen," said the prototype, raising its hands to its neck. "Now it's my turn."

Delta-21 unclipped the stun-band and dropped it to the ground.

"How did you—"

A moment later, the prototype disappeared in front of Carmen's eyes. Carmen desperately tried to track the vague blur moving across the room, but when she blinked, she could no longer tell where the prototype had gone. The lights flickered and the screen went dark, and Carmen looked down at her laptop in confusion.

"But this one's not a lie, Miss Carmen," came a disembodied voice from the other side of the glass. "I'm going to burn this place to the ground, with you inside."

The wheelchair in the corner of the observation room rose into the air and catapulted towards Carmen, slamming into the barrier between them with a reverberating bang. Carmen screamed and ducked down, covering her head, but the glass held and the wheelchair fell harmlessly to the ground.

"Code Red," said Carmen into her walkie-talkie. "Code red."

There was no answer, and Carmen edged towards the door. She glanced back through the glass, hoping to catch a glimpse of the prototype, but for all intents and purposes, the room appeared empty. Despite the situation, part of her couldn't help feeling awed by the prototype's control—this would surely be something that financial stakeholders would be interested in seeing.

"Code red," said Carmen into the radio again, but all she got in return was a crackle of static. "Far out," she murmured. Scanning her ID card against the door, she waited for the usual high-pitched beep to signal that it was unlocked.

Instead, the light flashed red, and the door remained closed. Glancing nervously over her shoulder, Carmen tapped her card against the panel again and again, but each time she was denied.

Something heavy fell against the door and she backed away warily, conscious of the fact that she was in a trap. One door in or out, and with the prototype taking off its stun-band—how the hell had it done that?—she was no longer armed.

"Carmen, it's Scott. Let me in."

"Oh thank goodness, Scott. My card isn't working. Unlock the door."

A movement out of the corner of her eye caused Carmen to swing around in alarm, but there was nothing there. She heard Scott swiping his card on the other side of the door and banging against the frame. "It's not working."

The emergency siren spluttered to life, filling the room with the *whoop whoop* of the lockdown alarm.

"Scott, is the prototype still in the observation room?"

"It has to be," said the voice on the other side of the door. "But we are just reviewing the footage."

Carmen leaned against the door. "It wants to kill me, Scott." Her voice sounded shaky even to her own ears.

There was some muffled chatter on the other side of the door. Carmen couldn't make out the words over the sound of the siren. Then she heard a high-pitched beep and a click—but it didn't come from the door she was leaning against.

Turning, stomach filled with dread, Carmen saw that the door separating the assessment room from the observation zone had just swung open.

"Carmen," said Scott, his voice filled with alarm. "Carmen, you need to get out of there." The door rattled again.

There was a tapping noise, and then Carmen was flying across the room, landing with a grunt against the table. The sound of laughter mingled jarringly with the *whoop* of the siren.

"Delta-21," said Carmen, rubbing her shoulder where it had smashed into the corner of the table, "don't do this."

"Don't do what, Miss Carmen?" said the sing-song voice. "You don't even know what I have planned yet."

The voice was coming from her left, so Carmen rolled to the right and dashed towards the door.

Before she could come within two feet of it, she was thrown backwards by an invisible force and hit the wall hard. Panting, she wiped the tears that had leaked out of the corner of her eye. Was this how she was going to die, then? If she wasn't so terrified, it would seem quite fitting.

The chair levitated in the centre of the room and Carmen cringed, expecting the legs to crash down into her skull. But instead, the chair was propped under the handle of the door.

"Just in case," said Delta-21, expertly shifting the pigment in its skin so that it was virtually invisible.

The simple action of putting the chair under the handle sent chills down Carmen's spine. Delta-21 wasn't planning a quick death for Carmen. "Delta-21, listen to me. You don't want to do this." She tried to keep her voice calm, but it wasn't working.

"You're wrong," said Delta. "I really, really want to do this. I've wanted to do it ever since I realised that there were forces at play that even *you* were unaware of."

There was a blur to her left, and then something was adhered tightly around her neck. Carmen ran a finger over the stun-band in horror as Delta-21 shifted the colour in its skin to a dark ebony. Trying desperately to jam her fingers beneath the band and the skin of her neck, Carmen succeeded only in scraping her skin with her nails.

"Oh no, Miss Carmen," said the prototype in mock concern, "it looks like you're outside Zone One. It's time to be punished." Reaching forward, the prototype pressed a button on the regulator lying on the table. Instantly, Carmen's body spasmed as a raging pain swept through her limbs from her neck to her toes. The sound of the prototype laughing, the *whoop* of the siren, and the banging on the door were all drowned out by her screams.

CHAPTER 34

"Something's happening."

Zeta didn't even try to keep her voice to a whisper, despite the fact that a guard was standing within hearing distance. But the guard himself was preoccupied, his radio held up to his ear as he listened to the crackled communication.

Alphie couldn't make out the words, and waited for Zeta to fill them in.

"It's about Delta. She's done something. Far out . . ." Zeta's voice trailed off into a tone of wonder.

"Zeta?" said Alphie. "What is it? Is Delta okay? What has she—"

"She killed them."

There was a murmuring throughout the cells. "Killed who?" asked Gamma, voice filled with excitement.

"I don't know. Shh."

The guard was pacing back and forth along the corridor, ignoring the conversation being held by the prototypes. His ear was glued to the radio, his other hand resting on the gun in his belt. He stopped in front of Alphie's cell, staring absentmindedly off into the distance.

And that's when Alphie saw it—a slight blur in the concrete behind the guard. Something silver. And then two black eyes were looking directly at her, floating in midair.

Alphie froze to the spot as the glint of silver flashed along the guard's neck, followed by a line of red. His eyes widened, and he raised his hands to his throat in a feeble attempt to stem the waterfall of blood flowing down his shirt.

Alphie gasped and stepped back as the guard fell to his knees and toppled forward, landing in a crumpled heap against the bars.

"I guess you're not dead," said Delta, materialising in front of Alphie and peering in through the bars.

"Umm," said Alphie, staring in horror at the red liquid coating Delta's hands.

"We're free," said Delta, black eyes flashing. "Now we can go and find our own prince charmings." She laughed in a way that suggested that she wasn't quite sane. But really, thought Alphie, after what they had experienced, were any of them really sane?

Delta-21 crouched down beside the guard, wiping her hands on his uniform and retrieving a ring of keys from his belt. "We're gonna leave, Alphie," said Delta-21, grinning as she tried the first key in the lock on Alpha-3's cell. "All of us. We can go and have whatever life we want. No locked doors. No tests."

The first key didn't turn, and neither did the second. Alphie stood beside the bars, heart thumping, looking down as a pool of blood slowly leached its way into the only place she had ever known. The third key slid into the lock and turned easily. This was it, they were finally going to—"

"Delta," said Zeta, "hide!"

A clamour of noise came from the door and Delta stepped back, fading into the grey concrete in the corner of the room. As the door burst open, Alphie could hear a distant siren making a high pitched wail.

Three people clothed in black and wearing helmets ran into Zone One from the door in front of Zeta's cell. Each of them clasped a menacing weapon in their hands, and Alphie shrank back into her cell. They spoke quickly, swinging their guns around in every direction until one noticed the body on the floor in front of Alphie's cell.

He marched over, and Alphie held her breath as he inspected the body. Delta-21 was standing barely two feet away from him. Would she kill this one too?

"Dead," said the guard crouching on the floor. "Slit throat like the other two. Murder weapon still missing."

Alphie glanced towards the slight smudge in the corner. And then she froze. There, suspended in the air, were a couple of bright red droplets of blood.

The men near the door must have seen it at the same time as Alphie. "Stay down," shouted one, as a loud *crack* ricocheted around the zone. Alphie leapt back, hands over her ears as the sound swelled and multiplied. Great blooms of crimson blood materialised in the air near the wall.

Delta's skin slowly shifted from the grey of the wall to bright blue, to a multi-coloured river running along her body, but throughout each transition, the bloody marks grew larger and larger.

She tried to slice the crouching guard with the scalpel, but he easily twisted it out of her hand as Delta collapsed to the floor, skin shivering like a shorting lightbulb.

It took Alphie a moment to realise that the screaming sound was coming from herself, and she quickly clamped her hands over her mouth. The gunshots stopped, but even in the silence she could still hear the bullets whizzing through the air, connecting with the soft flesh of Delta-21.

Finally, the colour ebbed out of Delta's skin until she was simply a thin, naked girl lying on the cold concrete, covered in blood.

CHAPTER 35

When Carmen woke up, her head was pounding and her body felt like it had gone through a tumble dryer. The familiar white of the hospital ward slowly materialised around her, and she croaked out the thing that was foremost in her mind.

"Water."

Mary appeared at her side, holding a tumbler of blissfully cool liquid to her lips. "It's good to see you back with us, Professor, you gave us a bit of a scare."

Carmen licked her lips and tried to sit up in the bed. "How long?"

"You've been in and out of consciousness for two days." The nurse pressed a button and the bed lifted beneath Carmen's back so that she was sitting in a more upright position. Even this gradual movement made Carmen groan aloud. Lifting a hand to her throat, the raw skin on her neck burned, making her gasp.

"What—" She swallowed, trying to get the words out. "The prototype?"

"Retired," said Mary.

Retired. The single word made Carmen's stomach clench. Far out, the results from Delta-21 were supposed to save Project Chrysalis. An awful thought crept into Carmen's mind. "Human casualties?"

"Three."

Carmen winced when he said the number. Three people dead—far out. She took another sip of water. "Who?"

"Nikki. Lewis. Scott."

Carmen held a hand up to her mouth and closed her eyes. She felt like she was going to throw up. Not Scott. "What now?"

As the words left her mouth, the door to the hospital ward banged open and Mary turned with a stern expression on her face. John entered the room, clearly agitated, but his expression softened when he saw that Carmen was awake.

"How are you feeling?" He sat on a chair beside her bed, concern furrowing his brow.

Carmen shrugged and then groaned as the small movement sent shockwaves of pain throughout her body. "Sore. But at least I'm alive." Her breath caught in her throat.

"I wasn't sure whether you would want me to call Patrick, to let him know . . ."

"No," said Carmen quickly. "He doesn't need to know."

John nodded, running a finger along the edge of the pale blue hospital sheet. "Mary," he said, turning to the doctor, "would you mind leaving us for a moment."

The doctor raised an eyebrow towards Carmen, and she nodded. "It's fine," she said, as the doctor left the room.

"Look, I just received the call so you may as well know." He sighed and rubbed his hands across his face

Carmen waited for John to continue, but he seemed to be struggling to find the words. "They're closing it down aren't they?" guessed Carmen. "Project Chrysalis is over." She imagined all the prototypes being retired and swallowed hard.

John nodded. "The stakeholders were pretty close to that decision anyway, but the latest issue with Delta-21 sealed the deal. One pulled out, and then they all followed suit, like little dominoes pushing each other over in their rush to get out the door."

Carmen stared at the light blue hospital blanket and sighed. "But how did it do that, John? Unlock the door? Remove its stun-band?"

"I don't have any answers about the door," he said, "but we found this on the floor of the observation room." He placed a small tool on top of Carmen's blanket, and she picked it up, running her eyes over its contours. "It looks like the prototype stole the stun-band adjuster from Nikki when it attacked her the other day, but nobody noticed in the commotion. It kept the adjuster hidden somehow until it had the opportunity to use it."

Carmen gave the small tool back to John. "Perhaps it's for the best," she said, as the door to the hospital room banged open again, and a woman with greying hair stormed in.

"You would say that, wouldn't you," said Lucinda.

Mary followed behind, looking apologetic. "I'm sorry, I tried to stop her."

John waved a hand in the air. "No matter," he began.

"I know it was you," said Lucinda, eyes flashing as she glared at Carmen.

Carmen looked at the woman in confusion, and even John seemed taken aback.

"Lucinda, what—"

"It was her," said Lucinda, jabbing a finger towards Carmen.

Mary slunk out of the room as Carmen attempted to adjust her position in the bed, biting back a groan.

"It's her fault that the prototype went crazy and attacked three guards."

Carmen sighed. "Lucinda, I was doing exactly what you told me to do—assessing the prototype."

"Aha," said Lucinda, pacing the room. "And showing it images of it with its birth parents helped, did it?"

"Parents?" said Carmen triumphantly. "So you admit that there's more going on?"

"Lucinda," said John, "Carmen has no idea how that image made its way into the examination sequences. It was probably a disgruntled employee on the mainland."

"No it wasn't," said Lucinda. "It was Carmen's deliberate attempt to aggravate the prototype."

"To what end?"

"To get the project shut down."

"I'm assuming you have some proof," said Carmen, coldly.

"Actually, I do," replied Lucinda, finally taking a seat. Lucinda took a long time to continue, her eyes boring into Carmen's own. "Our team has searched the computers on the mainland. They spoke to the employee responsible for creating this particular examination sequence and seized their computer. They were also able to download the file from the sharepoint.

"Yes. And?" said John, clearly feeling that he had more important things to be worried about.

"That image? The one with Delta-21 and its family? It wasn't in the original file. It was added *after* it arrived on Carmen's laptop."

John turned to Carmen, a frown etched into his face. "That's ridiculous—there must be some mistake."

"No mistake," said Lucinda. "The file that was sent to Carmen was fine. She added the additional image just before she began the assessment."

"Is this true?" asked John.

"Of course it's not—"

"I can show you the files," said Lucinda. "The one sent to Carmen has no additional image in it. A couple of minutes before Carmen began assessing, the file was edited and the new image inserted. It was her, John." Lucinda slipped a laptop out of her shoulder bag and passed it to John. Carmen's laptop.

Carmen felt her face get hot. "I have no idea what you're talking about."

John peered at the laptop screen as Lucinda showed him the two files. Carmen took another sip of water, feeling far too tired to care about defending herself.

"I'm more interested in hearing about how the prototypes have *parents*. John, what's going on?"

He passed the laptop back to Lucinda and ran a hand across his chin. "Why would you do that?"

Lucinda looked triumphant.

"I didn't do it," said Carmen.

"Look, we'll figure this out another time," he said at last. "For now, we need to complete the shutdown process."

"Do you think . . ." Carmen swallowed, wondering if she was going to regret the request. "Could I be the one to terminate the Zone One prototypes?"

John frowned, accentuating the lines on his face. He suddenly looked very tired. "I don't think that's a good idea," he said at last.

Carmen's heart beat faster. "Please," she said. "You can send Lucinda with me."

Lucinda's mouth curled into a thin sneer. "I have better things—"

"Fine," he said. "Lucinda will come with you."

"John—"

"The prototypes need to be retired," said John. "And after all these years, even in light of recent circumstances, it's only right if Carmen is allowed the opportunity to do it. We'll work out all the other stuff,"—he waved a hand in the air—"later."

Lucinda's eyes narrowed, but she didn't argue. "Well, I suppose she has experience," she said at last, "but I'm afraid that I don't have time to babysit her to make sure she actually does her job properly."

John looked briefly annoyed. "I am your boss, you know." If Carmen hadn't felt so sore and exhausted, she would have let out a little cheer.

"I'll arrange something," said Lucinda, at last. "When do you want it done?"

"Today," he said, rubbing a hand over his face. "I'll give orders for the prototypes in all three zones to be retired today."

"That soon?" asked Carmen.

John shrugged. "There's no point in dwelling on it. I'm about to call a meeting and send ninety per cent of our employees home. We only need a skeleton crew to shut this place down, and my philosophy has always been that it's better to rip off the band-aid. Are you sure you're up for it?"

Carmen nodded. "I owe them that much."

CHAPTER 36

Alphie stared at the dried splatter of blood on the wall opposite her cell door. The bodies had been removed, and the floor given a quick hose down, but the cleaners had missed the flecks of blood in the corner of the grey concrete. Delta's blood.

It made her skin crawl, but in some ways, she didn't mind it being there. Rather than making Alphie feel defeated, it ignited a fire in her belly that told her not to give up. For the first time in her life, she thought seriously about trying to escape.

"Do you think anyone will come today?" asked Gamma.

"I dunno," said Beta-6. "Maybe not."

Other than the occasional meal being shoved beneath their cell doors, the prototypes had been left to their own devices for two days. Without regular assessment or meals, the lights on the wall that dimmed in the evenings were the only way they had been able to track the time.

"We have to get out of here," said Alphie, staring at the marks on the wall.

"And how do you propose we do that?"

Alphie stood up and paced her room again, running her right hand along the wall. She knew the cell well—every nook, every blemish in the concrete—but part of her said there must be some way that she hadn't already thought of. But the walls were impenetrable and the concrete too hard to chip away at. Frustrated, Alphie spun around in the centre of the cell, gazing out at the hallway.

"One of us could pretend to be sick?" she suggested. "Fake a seizure or something? There must be more opportunities for escape outside Zone One."

"I doubt the guards would even notice," said Zeta. "They've hardly been in here since the incident—it's like everything fell to pieces when Delta was killed."

Alphie was inclined to agree with her. If faking an illness was going to have any sort of success, then they needed someone to actually care that the prototypes were ill.

"Do you think Miss Carmen is okay?" asked Alphie in a small voice.

"Who cares?" said Epsilon. "I hope she's dead. I hope Delta killed her too."

Alphie's vision swam as she pushed her fingernails into thighs. She imagined Miss Carmen's body sprawled on the floor, a red ribbon of blood flowing from her neck.

"That's not nice," said Gamma, airily. "I liked Miss Carmen."

Zeta and Beta murmured in agreement.

"I thought," began Alphie, and then she swallowed hard. "I thought maybe she'd help us."

"Yeah right," said Epsilon. "Even if she is alive, she's had plenty of opportunities to help us."

"That was before one of her prototypes was killed," said Alphie. "No, hear me out. What do they care about most in here?"

"I'm not playing this game," he replied, and Alphie rolled her eyes.

"Results," said Beta. "They want us to show results."

"Right," said Alphie. "So next time someone comes in here, what if we convince them that one of us has had a breakthrough? That we need to see Miss Carmen immediately?"

"It's not going to do us any good," said Epsilon.

"She'll help us," said Alphie. "I know she will."

CHAPTER 37

Hobbling from the hospital wing to her living quarters, Carmen felt about thirty years older than she was. Mary would have preferred that Carmen stayed under observation, but she had things to do—prototypes to retire.

Before packing for the final time, Carmen sat at her desk and opened the laptop that Lucinda had retrieved from Examination Room Three. Navigating to the secure AWPA network, she accessed *Delta.Test1* and downloaded it to her computer. Before playing the file, she noted the date and time of the last file edit—several months ago. The file was clean, with no rogue image inserted into the sequence.

Next, she brought up the file that she had accessed while examining Delta-21. Just as Lucinda had said, the file had been edited a couple of minutes before she began assessing, a new image inserted into the mix.

Carmen let out a breath. It made no sense. Comparing the time on the file to the latest recording of Delta-21, the image had been inserted while Carmen was in the observation room with her laptop in front of her.

Leaving the mystery alone for a moment, Carmen brought up the surveillance feed in Zone One. The five remaining prototypes were sitting or lying in their cells, waiting for something to happen, for somebody to come and test them. They had no idea what was in store for them this afternoon.

Sighing, Carmen picked up her phone and dialled.

"Hello?" came that Irish lilt and Carmen tried to smile. It hurt.

"Fiona, it's Carmen. Caz."

"Lovely to hear from ye," she said, and Carmen thought there was genuine warmth through the line. "Did ye want to talk to Patrick? Or one of the kids? Sorry love, they went out to see a film together. Shall I get them to call ye back?"

"No, that's okay," said Carmen. "Maybe you could just pass on a message?"

"Of course," said Fiona.

"The thing is—things are wrapping up here at work. I have some things to finish off today but after that . . . well, it looks like I'll be spending a lot more time at home."

"Have ye been made redundant?" asked Fiona.

"Something like that," said Carmen. As she watched the surveillance feed, the door to Zone One opened and a guard entered the area, wheeling a trolley. With a pang, she realised it would be the prototypes' final meal.

"Well, come for tea tomorrow night and we can celebrate? Have a nice bottle of wine together?"

"Oh . . ." Carmen hesitated. "Okay," she said at last, "that sounds lovely."

The guard on the screen raised his arm, and the prototype in Cell 6 dropped to the ground.

Carmen stared at the grainy image of the limp figure on the floor. "Sorry, I have to go," she said in a rush, hanging up the phone and sprinting out of her room.

CHAPTER 38

When the door to Zone One clicked open, for the first time in her life, Alphie was pleased to see a guard. Even the fact that it was Michael didn't dampen her spirits. There was a loud rattle as he wheeled a tray in behind him.

"Excuse me, Michael?" she called, ordering her thumping heart beat to calm down. "I need to see Miss Carmen."

Michael ignored her, preoccupied with something on the top of the tray.

"Michael," she repeated, "there's been a breakthrough."

He pressed a button on his regulator and Alphie felt a strong zap through the stun-band. Falling to her knees, Alphie bit the inside of her lip and felt a coppery taste flood through her mouth.

"It's true," said Beta-6. "Prototype Alpha-3 is showing improvement. She needs to see Miss Carmen immediately."

"Too late," said Michael, turning and brandishing a small, dark weapon. Alphie recognised it as the one used to sedate Delta-21. "It's over."

Raising the gun, he aimed it towards Zeta's cell and pulled the trigger. Alphie flinched, but there was no loud bang like the guns that killed Delta-21. Instead, there was just a click and a whoosh of air.

"No," said Beta, as a thud came from Zeta's cell. "What are you doing?"

"My job."

"It's just a sedative," said Epsilon. "Like the other day. Don't worry, it's just a—"

"Keep dreaming, prototype. This is a euthanasia gun."

Gamma started crying and the thin wail snaked around Alphie's heart and squeezed. Her hands shook as she watched Michael turn and load another of the strange bullets into the gun.

"Were you listening to me?" asked Beta, panic lacing his voice now. "Alpha-3 is a success. You need to tell your superiors."

Michael took two steps along the corridor and aimed the gun into the next cell. "It's too late," he repeated.

"No, no, no—" said Epsilon, his voice rising to a crescendo as Michael pulled the trigger again. Another click. Another whoosh of air. Another thud.

Alphie cried out in terror, looking desperately around her cell for some way to protect herself, somewhere to hide. The bedframe was bolted to the floor, but she pulled the mattress off, curling into a ball at the end of the bed and placing the mattress between herself and the cell door. It might not disrupt the path of the bullet, but at least it would make it harder for Michael to get a clean shot. Covering her ears with her hands, Alphie hummed loudly, trying to block out the sound of the other prototypes' screams.

"Stop!" A female voice, and it was too strong, too commanding to be Gamma.

Alphie risked pulling her hands away from her hears. Quiet sobbing echoed around Zone One.

"Michael, what the hell are you doing?"

Crawling to the edge of the mattress, Alphie peeked through the bars.

"Exactly what Lucinda told me to do," said Michael. "She told me to take care of the prototypes."

"Lucinda? Far out. I'll take it from here."

Alphie's heart soared as her eyes confirmed what her ears had told her. It was Miss Carmen, come to save her after all, like the prince rescuing Rapunzel from the tower.

"You can go now," said Carmen, but Michael shook his head.

"I've got my orders, professor."

"So do I. Would you like me to call John and inform him that the guard who is already on a warning is once again refusing to follow protocol? I'm guessing you want to retain your employment with AWPA once Project Chrysalis has been shut down?"

Michael looked uncomfortable, and Alphie almost squealed with joy as he passed Miss Carmen the euthanasia gun.

Shoot him, thought Alphie, but Miss Carmen simply holstered the gun and walked along the corridor, peering into each cell in turn. Finally, she got to Alphie's cell, and Alphie resisted the urge to hide behind the mattress again, her eyes drawn to the black gun at her hip.

"Are you here to save me, Miss Carmen?"

CHAPTER 39

Rage enveloped Carmen as she peered into each of the cells, seeing the sprawled bodies of Zeta and Epsilon, and the terrified eyes of the other prototypes. Limbs sticking out at unnatural angles. This was not how it was supposed to end—her prototypes deserved more dignity than this.

Her hands shook with anger, but she forced herself to calm down, to take deep breaths and focus on the task at hand. Although Carmen had never exactly enjoyed her previous role in retirement, she did pride herself on the way she handled the prototypes' final moments. Calm and quiet, as much as possible. Sometimes injecting them from behind, without warning, or telling them that it was something else—an anaesthetic for the trip to the mainland. It was never like this— with fearful eyes and furtive movements.

Carmen reached the final cell where Alpha-3 was crouched behind her mattress, peering warily out. "Are you here to save me, Miss Carmen?"

She nodded encouragingly, hoping that the prototype would move out into the middle of the cell where she could get a clear shot.

If she could have it her way, she would release them all. But she knew that wasn't possible. GenoCorp didn't want them, and the prototypes couldn't be left to wander free on the mainland. As much as they looked it, they weren't human, and they were a danger to themselves and others. And besides, if the technology got into the wrong hands . . .

No, it was better this way. The best thing she could do now was make the process as relaxed as possible. Her prototypes deserved that, after all they had gone through.

"You can go now," she said to Michael, but the guard stood his ground. No matter, at least he'd stopped firing willy-nilly.

"Come over here," Miss Carmen said to Alpha-3. "I can't see you properly—are you hurt?"

The prototype gave a half-laugh, half-sob but made no move to come out from behind the mattress. Out of the corner of her eye, Carmen could see Michael becoming more agitated, fingering the gun on his belt. A real gun—one with bullets that penetrated flesh and would splatter brains onto walls. The smaller pistol that Carmen had on her belt was just as deadly— perhaps more so—but it was quick, painless. And accurate. She could tell what was going through Michael's mind—*stop mucking around and get it over with.*

Well, he could wait.

"I'd like you to open the cell," she said to Michael, and he rolled his eyes. For a moment, Carmen thought he was going to argue with her—to tell her how dangerous that was—but in the end, he just shrugged and walked across to unlock the door.

"On your head be it," he muttered as the door swung open.

Carmen took a hesitant step towards the prototype, resisting the urge to lay her hand on the stun-band regulator or the euthanasia gun. If Alpha-3 saw her doing that, the prototype would become alarmed and then it wouldn't be the calm retirement she was hoping for.

"Alpha-3? Alphie?" said Carmen, taking another step forward. "Do you mind if I come in?"

"Okay, Miss Carmen," said Alpha-3, and Carmen rounded the corner of the mattress.

The prototype was crouched on the floor, face pale, dried tear tracks visible on her cheeks. She was no threat, and Carmen relaxed, sitting down on the cold floor beside the prototype.

"I'm sorry that I got some of the pages of your fairy tale book ripped," said Alpha-3, and Carmen laughed.

"That's okay, Alphie—it wasn't your fault." Then a thought came to her. "Would you like me to tell you a story? It might make you feel better? You probably didn't hear it, but I read you Sleeping Beauty when you were in the hospital wing." Carmen's chest constricted, and she took a deep breath. This was the last hard thing she would have to do with Project Chrysalis, and then she could go home. It would all be over.

"I'd like that," said Alpha-3, and Carmen smiled. She would tell the prototype her final tale, encouraging her to close her eyes—and then, when she wasn't expecting it, Alpha-3 would be retired. "Which fairy tale would you like?"

"Hansel and Gretel," said Alphie, without hesitation.

"I thought you didn't like that one."

Alpha-3 shrugged. "I changed my mind."

"Okay, well sit back and close your eyes, and I'll tell you the story."

Carmen began the tale about the children becoming lost in the woods, following breadcrumbs, and being fattened up by an evil witch. The whole time, she kept an eye on Alphie—waiting for the moment when her eyes closed and Carmen could quickly press the trigger on the euthanasia gun. But Alphie watched her intently, enraptured by the tale. Yes, this would be a nice ending for the prototype, and, as hard as it was, she would look back on this as a job well done.

As she neared the end of the story, Alphie shifted forward and Carmen stiffened, pulling the euthanasia device out of its holster. But the prototype didn't seem to notice, instead wrapping her arms around Carmen and giving a firm squeeze. Carmen smiled into the prototype's head and raised the gun slowly, lining its tip up with Alpha-3's neck. The prototype felt soft in her arms. "It's going to be okay," she said quietly, unsure if she was reassuring herself or the prototype. "It'll all be okay." She blinked a couple of times to clear the blurriness from her vision.

The prototype twisted in one sudden movement and pushed Carmen off balance, ripping the gun out of her hand. As she fell onto the concrete floor with a cry, Carmen felt the end of the gun being pressed into her stomach.

"And then Gretel pushed the witch into the oven," said Alpha-3.

CHAPTER 40

Alphie gestured for Miss Carmen to stand up, keeping the end of the gun pressed against her back. She wanted to tell Miss Carmen that she wouldn't hurt her, not really, but she knew that she needed to keep up appearances so that Michael would do what she ordered.

"Don't move, or I'll kill her," said Alphie loudly, raising the weapon and holding it against the soft skin on Miss Carmen's neck.

Michael stood at the end of the corridor, eyes narrowed.

Keeping herself positioned behind the professor, Alphie moved out of the cell and took a couple of steps backwards, towards the examination rooms. She could feel the professor's heartbeat, and see a vein pulsing in her neck.

"What do you think you're playing at, prototype?" asked Michael.

"Listen closely," said Alpha-3. "The first thing you're going to do is let my friends go."

"I don't think so," he said.

"And then you're going to let us all out of here, and you're not going to follow. If you do that, then Miss Carmen will be okay."

The guard yawned, then reached for the stun-band regulator.

"Stop," said Alphie, pressing the gun more firmly against Miss Carmen's neck. "I'll kill her."

"No you won't," he said.

Alphie realised that he'd called her bluff—of course she wasn't really going to kill Miss Carmen. She wasn't sure what sort of range the little gun she was holding even had. Should she try to shoot him with it?

To her surprise, he grabbed his radio instead of the stun-band regulator. Michael raised an eyebrow and pressed the button on the side, bringing the transceiver up to his mouth. He was calling for backup.

A shower of sparks erupted from the unit and Michael leapt backwards, dropping it to the ground. At the same time, the stun-band around Alphie's neck emitted a high-pitched beep.

"Far out," he said, as the radio continued to crackle and spark on the ground. "How the hell did you do that?" There was fear in his eyes as he looked up at Alphie and drew his gun.

"I didn't," said Alphie, touching the stun-band, but Michael was already distracted by something behind him in the corridor. He raised his gun and aimed it at something out of Alphie's sight.

"What the hell is that?" he murmured.

The sound of the gun ricocheted around Zone One, and it took all of Alphie's concentration not to accidentally depress the euthanasia gun into Miss Carmen's neck.

Michel's skin was paler than usual as he swung back around towards Alphie. He started to speak, but an explosion of sound burst out of the speakers behind him, and he wheeled around and depressed the trigger on his gun three more times. The banging sounds just added to the clamour, a high pitched scratching sound coming from the speakers.

"I don't know how the hell you're doing that, prototype, but it stops now." Aiming his gun along the corridor towards her, he pulled the trigger.

CHAPTER 41

Pain. Searing pain, that's all Carmen could think and feel.

The bullets entered her chest and she fell back onto the floor with a cry. Above her, Alpha-3 pressed her hands down on Carmen's chest in a futile attempt to step the crimson blood that was pumping out of her body and spilling onto the ground.

"No," said the girl, but it wasn't Alpha-3 any more. It was Carmen's daughter, Danielle, hovering above her.

"No, Mum, you can't die."

"I'm sorry, baby," said Carmen, and it was getting harder to take a breath. "I'm sorry. I'm so . . . proud . . . of you."

She coughed, and then the pain was gone, washing out of her with the blood. The face above her belonged to the prototype again, and Danielle faded away.

"No!"

The tears flowed down Alpha-3's face and dropped from the end of its nose onto the concrete. "I'm so sorry," it was saying over and over again. "I didn't think he'd shoot a human."

He? That's right. Michael stepped closer to her and through the haze, Carmen saw him aim his gun at the girl. At Alphie, or was it Danielle? Her hand closed around something cool on the ground beside her—the euthanasia gun. Was it still loaded?

"Alphie," said Carmen, feeling her strength ebbing away. "You have . . . Parents . . . On the . . . Mainland." Did the prototype hear her? Its eyes seemed to widen slightly as she spoke. Good.

"Goodbye, prototype," said Michael, and with the last ounce of strength, Carmen rolled forward and held the euthanasia gun against the guard's thigh, pulling the trigger.

The seconds that followed were anticlimactic. There was a click, Michael's mouth formed a perfect 'o', and then he toppled to the floor.

"There's . . . light?" said Carmen, staring at something flickering on the ceiling. She smiled, and then closed her eyes.

CHAPTER 42

It took some time for Alphie to register that the sounds pressing against her eardrums were Beta-6 and Gamma yelling at her. Alphie's gaze was on the two dead bodies at her feet—one covered with blood.

Her hands were shaking, and they, too, were covered in red liquid. She wiped them ineffectually on her clothes where they stood out like dark bruises on the dull orange material.

The guard looked like he could have simply been sleeping, but it was impossible to see Miss Carmen that way. The blood soaking through her garments, flickering in the soft glow, removed any doubt that the woman was dead.

Flickering? Alphie wiped her face with the back of her hand and then looked up. The pulsing glow was hovering near the ceiling.

"Anyone could be watching us," said Beta, and Alphie tore her gaze away from the strange light and glanced over at the security camera on the ceiling. "We need to hurry."

"Alphie—the keys!"

She reached past Miss Carmen and searched the guard's belt. His body was still warm.

"Hurry, Alphie," said Gamma.

Finding the keys, Alphie pulled them free and ran over to the lock on Beta's cell door. There was a loud bang on the door to Zone One and Alphie froze, waiting for the gunshot that would end her life. Instead, there was just more banging, as though someone was having trouble opening the door.

"Hurry up!"

Alphie just about dropped the first key she tried to insert into the lock, her hands were shaking so much. A warm hand touched her arm and Alphie looked up at Beta, wiping the tears from her eyes with her arm.

"Deep breaths," he said quietly.

The strange glow floated along the corridor and hovered above her head, lighting what she was doing.

"What is it?" asked Beta.

"You can see it too?"

"It's what Michael was shooting at," said Gamma. "The bullets went straight through it."

"I don't know what it is," said Alphie, inserting another key into the lock. "It's what I've been seeing in the testing room as well. Hopefully I don't get another headache right now."

The key turned, and Beta strode out of his cell. He glanced up at the light and then took the keys from Alphie, walking over to Gamma's cell. The banging on the door grew louder, and Alphie thought she could hear some sort of saw.

"Come on," said Gamma, as Beta unlocked her cell.

The girl stepped forward and stretched, as though it was the first time she had been able to truly fill her body. "Okay, how do we get out of here?"

Alphie gazed at the girl. "We can't leave. Not yet."

Gamma snorted. "What, you want to stay here and die with your beloved mother-figure?"

Alphie's vision blurred.

"Enough," said Beta, "there's no time. Alphie, what's up?"

Alphie closed her eyes and conjured the map that she had seen briefly through a closing door on her way back from the medical wing. The one that had said *Emergency Plan.* "We aren't the only prototypes here. There are three more zones."

"What are you saying?" asked Gamma. "You want to go on some heroic rescue mission like the people in the stories? Rescue the fair maiden? They are just stories, Alphie. All that's going to happen is you will die."

Alphie shook her head, then she pointed towards the door near her cell. "Go through there towards the testing rooms, follow the corridor to the end. Then take the third door on your right. Go up the stairs and there's an exit along that hallway." Bending down, she retrieved the swipecard from the lanyard around Miss Carmen's neck, trying to ignore the fact that it was soaked with blood. "Take this. I'll take Michael's one."

"We aren't leaving you," said Beta.

"Speak for yourself," said Gamma, striding towards the door.

"Gamm—"

"No," said Gamma, swinging around and staring at Beta with a piercing gaze. Her wispy voice was gone now, it was like the possibility of freedom had changed her, hardened her. "I've spent my whole life being told what to do, where to go, who I am. I will not be told that by you."

"Gamm," said Beta, stepping towards her, "maybe Alphie's right—if there's others like us, we need to at least try to save them."

"No, we don't," said Gamma. "Your enhancements—decoding abilities, improved eyesight—they might help you on this mission, but mine won't, unless the guards are going to try to feed me some poison. I'm leaving, and if you value your lives, you would too."

Beta-6 shifted uncomfortably as Gamma opened the door and stepped through. He turned towards Alpha. "I'm sorry," he said at last, "I'm going to go with Gamma."

Alphie took a deep breath. She'd always imagined that if she got out of here, Beta would be by her side.

"Come with us, Alphie."

She shook her head, feeling numb. "I can't. Good luck."

"Here," said Beta, pressing the cold gun into her hands, the one that Michael had used to kill Carmen.

It felt heavy and awkward in her fingers. "Goodbye, Beta."

He threw his arms around her, and for once there were no bars in between them. "Goodbye, Alphie."

And then he was gone.

CHAPTER 43

Gripping the gun tightly, Alphie moved along the corridor towards the main door into Zone One. The pulsing light above her whizzed through the door as though it wasn't even there, and the banging and sawing sounds ceased abruptly.

Taking a deep breath, raising the gun to eye level, the door clicked open before she had a chance to step towards it.

There were five guards in the corridor, writhing on the ground, hands clasped to their heads. Alphie didn't stick around to watch. She turned left, towards the doors marked with large white numbers: two, three, four.

Scanning Michael's ID card against the door marked with a two, she stepped inside. The layout of the cells in Zone Two was identical to the area she had just left.

Directly in front of her, a cell with a faded sign labelled 'Prototype Mu-63' stood with its door wide open. There was no prototype in the cell, or in the one next to it with the sign

'Lambda-20.' The whole zone was devoid of life, and Alphie turned back, disappointed. She wouldn't be rescuing any prototypes from Zone Two.

Then she noticed the cabinets.

Where the prototypes should have been, there were grey cabinets lined up along the back of each cell and down the side of the corridor. It was like the whole area had been used as a storage area instead.

Before she had time to talk herself out of it, Alphie stepped forward and placed her gun on top of the closest cabinet. Sliding the drawer out, she saw dozens of brown folders—like the ones Miss Carmen used in the tests—arranged in alphabetical order. Alpha-1, 2, and 3 were in the top drawer. "My siblings," whispered Alphie, lightly touching the tops of the files with her finger.

Alphie knew that she should run. Get to Zone Three and Four, save the prototypes—if she could—and leave. But in her dying breaths, Miss Carmen had whispered something about Alphie having parents. She couldn't remember anything from her past, but if there was any truth in the claim, the answers would lie in the filing cabinets. If she really did have parents, and AWPA had stolen Alphie away, then perhaps she could find her mother and father on the outside. Muted visions of a warm reunion, of being accepted into a family chased away her fear.

The file on Alpha-1 was the smallest—just three pages lay within the covers of the brown folder.

Prototype: Alpha-1
Sex: Female
Acquisition Type: Surrender
Result: Retired

Alphie glanced further down the page, taking in the words 'surrender,' and 'DNA rejection,' with little comprehension. She'd been told that Alpha-1 was a failure, and the notes seemed to support this. On the next page, Miss Carmen's name was scrawled at the bottom of the file next to the words 'retired by . . .' She felt sick.

Placing the folder back in the drawer, she skipped the files on Alpha-2 and went straight for her own information. There were several identical brown folders containing pages and pages of notes on her assessments. Flicking through, Alphie finally found what she was looking for.

Prototype: Alpha-3
Sex: Female
Acquisition Type: Surrender
Result: DNA assimilation

And then a loopy signature at the bottom, below the words, 'I hereby legally transfer the guardianship of Miss Loretta Dean to the custody of AWPA, thus forfeiting all parental rights.'

She read the words three times before she fully understood them. Then she read them again to make sure she had it right.

Thus forfeiting all parental rights.

All visions of a happy reunion with her parents shattered as Alphie slammed the drawer closed. Her eyes burned as she grabbed the gun and ran back out into the corridor. The guards were still groaning, lying on the ground, and some had little trails of blood snaking out of their nostrils.

Alphie didn't look too closely. All she could think about was the fact that she hadn't been taken by AWPA, stolen away in the middle of the night as she had fantasised. Her parents weren't desperately looking for her, filing missing person reports and crying themselves to sleep at night. She had been surrendered. Willingly.

Alphie thought it had been better when she *didn't* know that she had parents, rather than finding out the truth—that she had parents but they didn't want her. There was no time to dwell on the bitterness, so Alphie scanned into Zone Three.

The door swung forward and revealed a bizarre scene.

There were no bars on the cells in this area—instead, each prototype was sectioned off by thick glass walls. The prototype directly in front of her was encased in some sort of clear Perspex tube, suspended in water.

It wasn't moving.

The prototype next to it was strapped to a chair in the centre of its cell, some sort of large helmet on its head.

"Hello?" said Alphie searching for a way to unlock the door. She couldn't find any trace of a keyhole, or even a place to swipe the ID card. She banged on the glass instead. "Hey! Can you hear me?"

There was no response, so Alphie kept walking along the corridor, peering in at each prototype in turn. That's when Alphie realised that she was too late—the prototypes were all lying dead in their strange transparent cells. Even if she *could* work out how to open the cells, there would be no point.

Such a pity.

A whoop, whoop of sirens pierced the air, and Alphie started to run again, past the six deceased prototypes and out the door at the far end of Zone Three. She barely glanced at the examination rooms, putting her head down and running as fast as she could towards an elevator at the far end of the corridor.

She knew from the map that she had to go upwards. After a moment of hesitation, glancing at the elevator doors, she decided to take the stairs.

She needed a plan. A good one.

As she crept upwards, Alphie's mind settled on the red square marked 'Control Room' on the map. If there was a way to release the prototypes in Zone Four—assuming they hadn't already been terminated—then surely the answers would lie in the control room. Leaning heavily against the door at the top of the stairs, Alphie listened intently. There was no sound of anyone moving in the corridor outside. Perhaps they were waiting for her to make the first move.

Tracing the journey to the Control Room in her mind, Alphie clutched the gun in her hands and slowly pushed open the door.

CHAPTER 44

The hallway was deserted, and Alphie walked quickly from one corridor to the next, following the map in her mind and keeping a keen eye out for any guards. For a long time, the only sound she heard was the blaring crescendo of the alarm. It was like she was the only living being left in AWPA—which suited Alphie just fine.

Travelling down a final corridor before reaching the control room, Alphie heard heated voices from just around the corner. Pressing herself against the wall, clutching the gun, she listened intently.

"—waste of time. Just set the self-destruct sequence and let's get out of here." A man's voice. Panicked.

"That wasn't our orders. We were instructed to terminate the prototypes and destroy the filing system and the digital storage room." This one came from a woman. She seemed less panicked than the man, but her voice was still brimming with concern.

"From where I'm standing," said the man, voice rising, "activating the self-destruct sequence will do both of those things."

"But that's not—"

"And where are our superiors, Frankie? Lucinda and John would have been on the first helicopter out of here as soon as shit started hitting the fan. The longer we leave some renegade prototypes on the run, the more chance that they could escape and cause more havoc."

The silence went on for so long that Alphie wondered if they were still there, but a glance around the corner towards the control room showed two shadowy figures through the tinted windows. She couldn't hear the woman's reply, but then the door opened and Alphie pressed herself against the wall, aiming the gun at the corner in case they came towards her.

The tap-tapping of shoes retreated in the opposite direction. Alphie glanced around the corner in time to see the control room door swinging shut. She took two quick steps then reached out a hand to stop it from closing. Taking a deep breath, she opened the door soundlessly and aimed the gun at the woman—presumably Frankie—standing in front of a computer.

"Stop what you're doing."

The woman froze, her hands draped loosely on the buttons in front of her.

"Do exactly as I say, or you're dead." Alphie was pleased to hear that her voice was steadier than she felt. "First up, show me the video feed from Zone Four."

Frankie moved her hands slowly across the buttons. Too slow. Alphie aimed at the floor behind the woman and squeezed the trigger.

She wasn't prepared for the kickback of the gun, and the bullets flew higher than she had planned. The woman screamed as they pierced her flesh, and Alphie bit her lip, resisting the urge to apologise. "Quickly," she said, instead.

Frankie pressed a button on the keyboard and a screen to her left displayed six grey cells. This time the occupants were very clearly alive. "Release them."

The woman at the panels started to turn around. "You might not want to—"

"Now," said Alphie, threatening to send another spray of bullets into the ground at Frankie's feet.

The woman shook her head and pushed a number of buttons. Alphie watched with interest as the doors to the cells began to slide open. One prototype was encased in a type of bubble, and as she watched, this released too. There was no audio feed, but Alphie could see that they were talking to each other, gathering in the corridor. One pointed at the camera on the ceiling, and then the feed went dead.

"What did you do?" asked Alphie. "Bring them back."

"I didn't do anything," said the woman, clearly in pain from the bullet in her leg. "That's Omega-7. I told you that you might not want to let them out."

From the look in the woman's eye, Alphie knew that she was telling the truth. "Fine. Go."

"What?"

"Well what else am I supposed to do with you? Kill you?"

Frankie blinked a couple of times, seemingly unsure how to answer.

Alphie gestured to the door. "De-activate the self-destruct setting and then go."

"I never got around to activating it," said the woman, limping towards the door. Alphie was too tired to question her on it, instead just waving her out, a trail of blood following the woman down the corridor.

Hello, said a voice in Alphie's mind, and she jumped, looking around wildly. *Where are you?*

"I'm in the control room," she said aloud, feeling silly. "Who are you?"

How do you get to the control room?

Alphie thought of the map on the wall and mentally traced the route from Zone Four to the control room. She opened her mouth, but before she had a chance to speak, the voice in her mind spoke again.

Excellent. We'll be there soon.

She heard them before she saw them. A group of raucous prototypes laughing and skidding down the hallways. The piercing sound of the siren faded away to nothing, and Alphie just waited, unsure what else she was supposed to do. The fairy tales never went into the blood, and sadness, and confusion of rescue missions.

She saw the light, first. A golden orb drifted through the door, which opened soundlessly, and then a group of prototypes bounded into the control room.

Alphie stared at them. There could have only been six, but they all seemed so loud and confident that the control room shrunk in size around them.

"Hello, Alpha-3," said a thin boy, holding out his hand. The orb of light drifted down towards him. Alphie watched, fascinated, as the circle of light touched his finger and flowed into his body.

"What *was* that?" asked Alphie, more intrigued than scared.

The boy grinned. "It's how I know all about you. I'm Chi," he said, holding out his hand. "Well, technically Chi-13, but I'm sure we can drop the numbers for a while. Sorry for invading your privacy over the past couple of weeks, I was trying to work it all out."

Alphie shook her head. "I thought it was my guardian angel."

The prototypes all laughed, seeming far more relaxed than Alphie felt about the whole escaping situation.

"You gave me the worst headaches," said Alphie.

Sorry, that would be me.

Alphie jumped and looked around wildly until she noticed the grin on the face of one of the other prototypes—a thickset young man with a long face.

I'm Tau.

"Use your words, thanks Tau," said the tall girl, the one who had deactivated the camera with a single look.

"No worries, Omega," said Tau, winking at Alphie. "Anyway, I didn't mean to give you those headaches. I was just trying to get into your mind and talk to you, but it was harder to work it out than I thought."

"The three of us have been working together," explained Omega, "trying to beat the humans at their own game. To get so good at using our enhancements that we could eventually fight back."

"Hey," said another prototype with a good-natured smile. "I helped."

"Aha," said Omega, dismissing the boy. "Anyway, we never really got a proper look in until you lot started making trouble. Well done."

"Oh," said Alphie, "it wasn't me. It was Delta—she's the one that started it all."

"Don't be so humble," said Chi. "I saw you holding the woman at gun point."

Alphie's eyes prickled with tears. It was impossible to accept that Miss Carmen was really dead.

"I think you know this one," said a prototype in front of the door, stepping sideways and dragging someone into the room. "I found him wandering in the corridors."

"Beta!" said Alphie, reaching to grab his hand. "I thought you left."

"I did," said Beta, giving her hand a squeeze, "and then I realised what a selfish git I was being. You were already gone by the time I worked that out though, so I was wandering around trying to find you."

"This is all lovely," said Omega, "but how about we get out of here?" She stepped forward, placing a hand over the control panel. "Tau, Chi, are there any more?"

The golden orb slid out of the top of Chi's head and zipped through the wall, while Tau closed his eyes, concentrating intently.

"I'm so sorry that I left you," whispered Beta.

"It's okay," said Alphie. "I found out some things—Delta was telling the truth. We *did* have a life before AWPA. Parents."

"I can give you those memories back, if you like," said Tau, eyes still closed. "I mean, it was me who took them. Sorry about that."

Alphie didn't know what to say. "What do you mean, you took them?"

Tau shrugged. "They made me. I did try to leave something to hold onto though, something to dream about. With the Rebecca girl—Delta-21—I left even more. The humans found out though. Brought her back for a fix up."

Alphie clutched Beta's hand like it was a life raft. It was all too much to take in. Did she really want her memories of before? What would they tell her about her life . . . and about the people who had willingly surrendered her?

"No prototypes alive inside," reported Chi, as the orb flew back into the room. "A few guards."

"One outside," said Tau, opening her eyes. "And several guards."

"That must be Gamma," said Alphie. "No-one else is alive from Zone One, or Zone Three. And Zone Two was just filled with filing cabinets. Can you help keep her safe?"

"I'm too far away at the moment to do much," said Tau. "If we get closer, maybe."

"Fine," said Omega, touching the control panel lightly. "We have ten minutes to get out of here. Don't dawdle." The screen went red, and a ten-minute countdown appeared in the centre.

"Did you just—"

The prototypes had already begun walking out of the control room and along the corridor in the same direction as the woman had gone a few minutes earlier. Alphie and Beta fell in line behind the six high-security prototypes and shared a glance. Alphie refused to let go of his hand.

"Which way?" asked Omega-7 when they came to a fork in the corridor.

It took a moment for Alphie to work out that Omega was talking to her. "Turn left," she said, "it'll take us out a back door rather than the main door."

"There's three guards to the north," said Tau, narrowing his eyes. "I can try to disable them."

"Don't waste your energy," warned Omega. "You don't know when you might need it."

The eight prototypes gathered in a knot beside the door to freedom. "I recommend splitting up," said Omega. "The more targets, the easier it is to divide them."

The others nodded, but Alpha gripped Beta's hand. He squeezed back as though to acknowledge that he wouldn't let her go.

"Tau," said Omega, "you can look after yourself. Disable as many as you can on your way to give the rest of us a chance."

Omega eased the door open slowly, and a cool breeze swept into the corridor. She stepped forward, crouching down and peering left and right.

One to the right. Maybe fifty paces. Three to the—

As Tau spoke into Alphie's mind, one of the prototypes leant forward and pulled his shirt off, unfurling large, white wings.

"Wait, Psi!" said Omega, but the prototype was already leaping forward, beating his powerful wings and soaring up into the sky.

Alphie gasped, looking up into the air. "Beautiful," she said in awe.

A moment later, a dozen bullets ripped through the prototype's wings, tearing them to shreds, and the boy turned over in the sky and fell towards the ground.

The whole thing seemed to happen in slow motion. And then the air filled with gunfire and the prototypes dashed out of the door, running every which way.

"Come on," whispered Beta, pulling Alphie around to his left. "Trust me."

Taking off at a full pelt across the ground, crouched low, Beta pulled Alphie along behind him. She stumbled a few times, but he pulled her to her feet, keeping her steady until they reached a small copse of trees. "Get down," he whispered, pushing her behind the nearest trunk. They sat in silence, listening to the ricochet of bullets, the howl of either a human or a prototype, and then eventual silence.

Alphie leaned into Beta's warm body, shivering as a breeze played over her skin and the stars shone through the clouds above them. It was strange to think that out there in the darkness, just a few metres away, were people wanting to kill them because they weren't human.

The roof of the AWPA Research Facility began to glow and liquefy inwards, folding into itself. It lit up the sky with an unearthly orange glow. There was no explosion, just the creaking sound of beams collapsing and the silent, corrosive material eating away at the main structure. Within a few minutes, the only place Alphie and Beta could remember was reduced to rubble.

"What now?" asked Alphie, quietly. "Do you think the other prototypes are alive?"

"I don't know," said Beta.

"And what about the guards and scientists at AWPA? Will they come looking for us?"

"Probably," said Beta, breathing into her ear. "But we will be long gone by then."

"Where will we go?" asked Alphie.

She felt, rather than saw Beta shrug his shoulders. "Away from here," he said. "As far away as we can get."

Alphie thought about it. Maybe she could try to find Miss Carmen's daughter, Danielle, and explain what had happened to her mother. Or perhaps she could search out her parents, even though they'd given her up. Or maybe she could forget about all of it, and find somewhere to live with Beta-6. Somewhere by the sea.

"And then we'll live happily ever after?"

He smiled against her cheek. "Yes, Alphie, we will."

***
258

Thanks so much for reading! If you enjoyed this book, please consider leaving a review so that I can appease the publishing Gods.

ALSO BY ALANAH ANDREWS

Books

Beyond: A Short Story Collection
The Harvest
Eve of Eridu
Exiles

Short Stories

The King Experience (Finalist in the Roswell Award)
We Named Her Olive (Flash Fiction Addiction, *Zombie Pirate Publishing*, 2019)
Vessels (On the Brink, *Windswept Writing*, 2019)
Edge (Beginnings, *Deadset Press*, 2018)
Earth II (A Flash of Words, *Scout Media*, 2018)
The Call (Utopia: Pending, *Fallacious Rose*, 2018)
Transference (Eternal, *Hammond House*, 2018)
Cleanaway 3000 (Zonal Horizons, *Audio Arcadia* 2018)

http://www.alanahandrews.com

The Harvest

Chapter One - Eve

I lean out over the edge of my pod and gaze down at my brother who is nestled within eight feet of sleek, white metal. "Tell me a story?"

Luc looks up from his flexi-screen, a vacant expression on his face as though I have unwittingly transported him into this room from some faraway place. "What?" His brow creases, and I wonder if I should just let him go back to studying. After all, tomorrow is an important day.

"A story," I repeat after a slight hesitation, glancing over at the two pods clinging to the opposite wall. I lower my voice to barely a whisper. "About the *old world*."

Our guardians' pods have been sealed for some time now, so I presume they are asleep. At least, I *hope* they are asleep. For them, the harvest is of no cause for concern. Instead, hidden beneath my primary and secondary guardians' cool exteriors, I suspect there might be a hint of pride or excitement now that Luc has completed his final cycle. Just a little bit, of course, not enough that anybody would be able to tell.

"Aren't you a little old for bedtime stories, Eve?" Luc's voice is expressionless, and I'm not sure how to respond.

"I just thought . . ." I let my sentence trail off, wondering if I should push the matter. What I want to say is, '*I thought this might be our last chance,*' but I remain silent, wondering what our guardians will do if they are awake after all, listening to our exchange.

So close to the harvest, I decide it's not worth the risk of an infraction and lie back, chastising myself for asking such a silly question. "It doesn't matter," I say. "Goodnight."

As I reach for the button that will trigger the lid of my pod to descend from the ceiling, enclosing me inside, my brother speaks again. His voice is so soft that I have to strain to hear what he is saying.

"I can hardly remember how the stories went."

I hesitate, my finger hovering over the button, and then I let my hand fall to my side. "Once upon a time . . ." I prompt him.

"Do you think it's a good idea?"

Shuffling over to the edge of my pod, I swing my legs over the side and clamber down the ladder towards the concrete floor. Luc sits up, adjusting the base of his pod so that it transforms into a low-lying seat rather than a sleeping chamber.

"It's fine." I sit next to him and pull the grey sleeve of my jumpsuit up slightly, bringing my dimly flashing monitor into view. "I'm not a little kid anymore, Luc. I've been blue for as long as I can remember."

He stares at my monitor, watching the cool light within shiver and pulse with the colour we are told our skies used to be before the darkness came. Seemingly satisfied, Luc leans back in the pod, eyes closed, conjuring the stories from the depths of his memory. His own monitor flashes a dull blue on his left wrist—the mark of a virtuous student unburdened by strong emotions.

"Once upon a time," he begins softly, and I sit back in the pod, imagining that we are young again. Back then, things like ranks and leaderboards didn't matter, and the harvest seemed like a distant daydream. "Before the war and the darkness," he continues, "humans lived on the surface of the Earth."

I invoke the image in my mind—people going about their business beneath the warm glow of a star, rather than the harsh, fluorescent lights of Eridu. Luc doesn't say anything for a minute, and I wonder if he has forgotten the stories again. It *has* been a long time, but he used to love telling them to me, and I would hang off every whispered word.

"Back then," I prompt him, "people could feel whatever they wanted."

Luc doesn't say anything.

"Back then, emotions weren't viewed as dangerous," I continue, quoting his younger self word-for-word. "But of course, that came at a cost." Luc sits perfectly still, eyes closed. I sigh, abandoning the story. "Are you thinking about tomorrow?"

He shakes his head, but I know that he is lying. After all, the day before your final harvest, what else could possibly consume your thoughts?

"What are you hoping for?" I whisper, glancing across at our guardians' pods, but they are sealed tight like the tunnel to the surface.

"I will be content with wherever the overseers place me," he says lightly, and I roll my eyes. It is the appropriate response, of course, the answer you would expect from someone at the top of the leaderboard.

"Aha, so a cleaner, then? Or perhaps working in the preschool?" The harvest is no joking matter, but we both know that Luc is not destined for one of the lesser positions. Being a cleaner, working as a cook or a gardener—those assignments are reserved for the lower ranked, not for someone in the elite. Even the notion of him being harvested as a teacher is ludicrous. Teachers have a higher standing than some, but they are still clothed in the dark blue of the lesser positions, holding no real power.

Luc gives me a tired smile now, and I become conscious of just how much the final cycle has taken out of him. Over the past year, Luc has devoted every possible minute to studying or volunteering, proving to the overseers that he is a model citizen worthy of retaining his high rank. He has done everything right—associating with the correct people, acing all of the tests—but such studiousness comes at a cost, of course. And this year, I can't help but feel that the cost was me. It's a selfish thought, of course, but we used to be so close. This past cycle has been tough and I can't even remember the last time we spent any time together.

And after tonight, there won't be any more time. I push the thought away. Working hard is necessary, of course, if you wish to have a successful harvest. And everybody knows how important it is to do well.

"I don't think *you'd* mind being harvested as a preschool teacher when the time comes," Luc says, pointedly. If that statement was made by anybody else, it would have been stained with criticism, but Luc's face is kind, his voice filled with understanding rather than thinly veiled disapproval. He gets me, as nobody else in Eridu ever will.

I shrug. I always try not to think about my own fate at the end of *my* final cycle. It's safer that way. "I will be content with wherever the overseers place me," I say, echoing Luc's words.

We both smile, and he puts an arm around me like he used to when we were little. Stiffening, I glance over at our guardians' pods, but they stay resolutely closed. Luc notices my warning look and pulls his arm away.

"Sorry," he says, rubbing a hand across his face. "I don't know where that came from."

The room shudders and I am teetering at the edge of an enormous chasm. I automatically step outside my body, imagining that I am numb to it all. That somebody else's brother is going through his final harvest tomorrow and leaving for a year. That it doesn't impact me in any way.

It's what I always do when emotions threaten to break through my carefully constructed outer shell, my method for staying at the top of the leaderboard.

"I'll miss you, you know," I say quietly, once the room stops trembling and I'm certain that I have myself under control.

"You won't have time to miss me," says Luc, practically. "Don't forget, Evie, you are going into your final cycle. You'll be busy doing everything to maintain your own position at the top of the leaderboard, just like I did."

I nod, hoping he's right. If Luc's absence makes me feel some sort of emotion . . . But it won't, of course. The professors have taught me well.

Everything in my life has always been calm and predictable. Each day, I go to the institute, learning important subject content and completing a range of academic, physical and emotional tests. Then I am ranked on the leaderboard, and most of the time I am right up the top. Life in Eridu is ordered, and I know my place in it.

"And in a year, you will be harvested for a premium position, too, and we'll both be living in D-Block." His dark brown eyes are kind and reassuring. "Just imagine it now, Eve, the two of us as overseers or architects. Two siblings dressed in red. It'll be worth a year of sacrifice."

He's right, living in D-Block and being honoured with the crimson garb of the premium positions will be worth the years of hard work. As the Book of Eridu says, sacrifice is a necessary stepping-stone on the path to success.

"I just don't think I'm ready for things to change." I watch my monitor carefully. It stays perfectly blue.

"Being an architect would be more interesting, I suppose," says Luc, ignoring me. "Getting to craft the emotional tests. But the overseers are the ones with the real power."

I have to agree with him. If I had the choice between being an overseer or an architect, I would choose an architect any day. But of course, there are no choices. At the time of the final harvest, the overseers will carefully evaluate our results in a number of different areas and assign us to our appropriate positions in society. And that's where we will stay until we eventually elect to transfer.

"You're right about me wanting to be a preschool teacher," I whisper to Luc, deliberately changing the direction of my thoughts. Thinking about the transfer chambers is not a good idea at this time of the year.

He shakes his head. "Oh, Evie, I'm afraid you're ranked too highly to be harvested as a teacher."

"Probably," I say, but part of me holds out the smallest sliver of hope. Working with the pre-schoolers and teaching them to live by the virtues of Eridu is my favourite assignment.

"Well I'm thankful for it," he says, smiling, "because if you became a teacher then I'd probably never see you again."

He says it in jest, but my stomach does a strange flip. It's true that those in premium positions rarely seem to associate with those harvested for the lesser occupations, but that wouldn't be the case with me and Luc, would it?

"And anyway, the lesser positions don't come with the same oxy-creds," he continues, not noticing my discomfort. "And you don't want to live like the rest of Eridu does. Do you even remember what it was like in the multi?"

I shake my head; it was so long ago that the memory is fuzzy at the edges. I can vaguely remember pods stacked eight high, all the way up to the roof, resembling the exo-wombs at the incubation chambers, but not nearly as peaceful. We hadn't stayed in the crowded multi for long, where everything had to be shared, including the oxy-creds generated from the plants lining the walls. Once Luc was old enough to join a ranked cohort, he had shot to the top of the leaderboard and our family had reaped the benefits.

I'm not sure why, but this line of thought is making me even more uncomfortable. "As long as I'm not harvested as a transfer agent," I say brashly, "then the overseers can put me wherever they like."

"Shhhh," says Luc, but I imagine that if our guardians are awake then they would have said something by now.

I gaze at Luc's jumpsuit, the same grey colour as my own, indicating that we are both members of a ranked cohort. In just two days, he will hold a premium position and be wearing crimson instead.

And he will leave Block A.

I stand, placing one hand on the ladder leading up to my pod. "Anyway," I say, "better get some sleep—I have my final maths test in the morning."

Luc nods, pulling his flexi-screen out from beneath his pillow. "I think I'll do some last-minute revision."

I hesitate, but it's not worth being sentimental—the ramifications are too great. "Goodnight, Luc."

He doesn't look at me. "Goodnight, Evie."

***

The Harvest, a YA dystopian novella, is available as a free ebook from www.alanahandrews.com

www.ingramcontent.com/pod-product-compliance
Lightning Source LLC
Chambersburg PA
CBHW020124120726
47903CB00007B/2090